Hallowmas 2

Black Springs Abbey

GLORIA PEARSON-VASEY

VICTORIA HALL
PRESS

Tellwell Talent
www.tellwell.ca

ISBN
978-0-2288-8844-4 (Paperback)
978-0-2288-8845-1 (eBook)

TABLE OF CONTENTS

Acknowledgements vii
One 1
Two 10
Three 17
Four 23
Five 30
Six 39
Seven 45
Eight 52
Nine 58
Ten 64
Eleven 71
Twelve 79
Thirteen 84
Fourteen 90
Fifteen 95
Sixteen 101
Seventeen 108
Eighteen 113
Nineteen 121
Twenty 128
Twenty-one 133
Twenty-two 138
Twenty-three 145
Twenty-four 151
Twenty-five 157
Twenty-six 162
Twenty-seven 167
About the Author 172

ACKNOWLEDGEMENTS

Black Springs Abbey is the sequel to the historical fantasy, *The Bells of Prosper Station.*

In preparation for the second book, I continued to research the culture and oil heritage of our area, this time focusing on Oil Springs, the community where it all began.

Along with the readers, historians, archivists and librarians acknowledged in the first book, I wish to thank those more recently involved in the creation of *Black Springs Abbey.*

Special thanks to Bonnie Pearson, Tom Pearson, Laurie Vasey and Joel Vasey who provided invaluable critiquing and suggestions.

I am indebted to Charlie Fairbank who patiently answered my questions and showed me the complexities of the Fairbank oilfields, to Cathy Martin who escorted me behind the scenes in the village of Oil Springs, to the writings of Patricia McGee, and for the assistance provided by Connie Bell and Jackie South of the Oil Museum of Canada.

I am grateful to my late husband, Jim, my companion on many research treks where we toured and took pictures, often returning to some places numerous times.

Thanks to Bob McCarthy for promoting our joint works of fiction in the tête-bêche print version commemorating the 150th Anniversary of Oil Springs.

And heartfelt thanks to you who read my books and share my flights of fancy.

One

The police cruiser slowed as it reached the flats nestled on both sides of Veterans Way. Tires crunching softly on gravel, it rolled down a steep slope into the northern section of the flats. It then came to a stop near a pond whose dark waters, though risen to their reedy high-water mark, were not overflowing as during the previous weeks of spring melt and April rains. In actuality, the pond was a bulge in a tributary of Bear Creek which twisted willy-nilly through the flats and beyond.

Stepping from his vehicle, the young constable shut the door with a deliberate thunk so as not to startle the solitary figure sitting on a bench at water's edge.

"Hi, Hilma," he said as he walked towards her.

"Did Mavis send you?" she asked without looking up, having sensed his arrival even before he turned off the main road.

"I haven't seen your grandmother today," he replied. "I was driving by and saw you down here. Thought you could use some company."

"Were you looking for me?"

"Might have been."

Although her heart did an involuntary flip, Hilma kept her feelings veiled.

Aloud she said, "Actually, I've had company."

"Oh?"

"There was a woman standing by the bridge holding out her arms beseechingly."

"Recently?"

"Just before you came. She had pale wavy hair and was wearing a flowered skirt and a loose grey shawl."

"Where did she go?"

"She sort of faded away."

"Like fog?"

"Pretty much — only faster. Oh, look! There she is again. Do you see her?"

The constable peered across the water in the direction of her pointing finger to where a covered bridge straddled the creek. Constructed several years ago from old barn board and supports from the original road, the bridge provided a popular backdrop for photographers seeking Bridgeview Park's rustic setting for portraits and wedding parties.

"I don't see anyone," he said.

"Never mind. She's gone now. Strange..."

"Was it some kind of ghost?" he asked cautiously.

"I don't know. I've never seen a person who fades in and out before."

"Did you really see her or are you teasing me," he said.

"I saw her," she insisted. "Don't look at me like that! You see auras don't you?"

"I expect most Sensos do," he said. "In my case, seeing a person's aura gives me an edge as a cop."

"Well, I don't see auras," she stated flatly.

"Really! I always assumed you did."

"I'm not gifted like my sister."

"You know that's ridiculous," said Garth. "Azur can't make a harp or cello sing like you can."

She knew this was true. She and her older sister, Azur, had both been exposed to music lessons as children, but whereas Azur soon found practice tedious, the younger girl was totally enchanted by the allure of music.

Hilma shivered as a breeze ruffled her shoulder-length hair.

"Are you okay?" asked Garth, knowing she wasn't.

"Not really. I'm a social outcast, a freak," she said.

Since her return to Providence Crossing after a year's absence, the townspeople seemed more wary of everyone known to carry the sensointuitive gene. Had they known of Hilma's adventure on the ghost train and her imprisonment by a psychic vampire they would have been even more mistrustful.

"Being a Senso gives one an advantage over other mortals," he said.

"It's fine for you to say. Most people seem to think Sensos are only female. They don't know that you're one."

"Azur and Dilly seem to have adjusted."

"They've got careers, husbands and children to distract them from their oddities."

"You could have that," said Garth.

"I'll always be the runaway who came back in withdrawal from some mysterious addiction."

"You're the only one obsessing on it, Hilma."

"The whole town knows about my unaccountable disappearance and that my grandparents kept me locked up for weeks after my return. The whole town knows that my physician brother-in-law supervised my rehab. The whole town knows that police were called to find me whenever I dared go walking by myself."

"You're exaggerating," said Garth. "And as far as the police go, Dr. XT always called me discretely. We were all on your side, *are* all on your side. We all know the hellish experience you'd been through."

"They should have left me in Vapourlea."

It had been five years since the intervention. Five years of hopeless dependency and frustrating uncertainty. Mercifully, the first year remained mostly a blur. Nursed back to health by Mavis, her determined grandmother, Hilma saw little of the townsfolk.

Her visitors during the lengthy withdrawal period were largely others who, like her, carried the inherited genetic factor: Azur, her friend, Dillian, and Garth who had just graduated from police academy. The only non–Sensos she saw then were her grandfather, Bram, Dr. Xavier Tennyson Barkley, now Azur's husband, and occasionally Dillian's husband, Graeme Kilgour.

Since that first hazy year, there had been glimmers of hope in the bleakness of Hilma's existence and sparks of joy interspersed between dismal stretches of days. Encouraged by family and friends, she completed a degree in the *Physics of Musical Sound* through online studies and occasional treks to the city for essential practicums, interviews and exams. On these occasions, she was accompanied either by her grandparents or Garth. While she reluctantly appreciated their dedication and patience, her need to rely on them rankled.

"Are you going to mope and feel sorry for yourself the rest of your life?" asked Garth.

She shot him an injured look and shrugged. "I came here this morning because I needed to walk off some energy, but I'm feeling chilled now. Would you mind driving me home?"

"At your service," he said, reaching for her hand and pulling her to a standing position. Still holding hands, they looked searchingly into each other's eyes. For a brief moment, Hilma allowed herself to imagine the feel of his tempting mouth crushing her own. Instead, she broke away and walked resolutely to the cruiser.

"Is there something you want to talk about?" he asked as he assisted her into the front passenger seat.

"I quit my music lessons," she said listlessly.

"Cello and harp both?"

Hilma nodded glumly.

"Why?"

"The teachers kept nudging me to perform publicly or take on some students of my own. I couldn't handle the stress of their expectations."

"I thought the purpose of the private lessons was to encourage you to share your musical talent with others."

"And to leave my cocoon," she finished for him. "Do you think I don't know that?"

Garth searched his mind for something appropriate to say and came up blank. Every time Hilma seemed to be making progress, she was gripped by fresh waves of anxiety and insecurities.

"Mavis and Bram haven't said much," she said, breaking the silence. "I know they're disappointed."

"There must be other options," he said.

"After what I've put everyone through, it would be ungrateful to fail totally. I've been trying to be boringly accommodating, but I can't seem to follow through with their plans for me."

"Perhaps their plans for you don't match your own."

Hilma sighed.

"Do you have time to go for a little drive?" he suggested.

"Anywhere in particular?"

"Black Springs Abbey," he said, turning the key in the ignition. "The abbess wants to speak with me, and I like to check on the place from time to time anyway since it's rather isolated."

"Isn't the abbess your great-aunt?"

"She is. Good old Aunt Jane."

"A ride would be a pleasant diversion," said Hilma. "Do I look okay for visiting nuns?"

Garth glanced over at the girl sitting beside him clad in blue jeans, pink running shoes and a knobby beige sweater.

"You look lovely," he said sincerely, bringing a blush to her pale cheeks.

The cruiser climbed up from the flats and drove through the streets of town into countryside vibrant with the greens of springtime. Despite her gloom, Hilma found herself relaxing as they headed south on the highway, passing trees lacy with unfurled leaves, others frothy with pastel blossoms.

"How many nuns live at the abbey?" she asked.

"Only seven now. Aunt Jane and three other old nuns - a porter, a cook and an organist. Then there's a lawyer in her early forties who joined the order after she already had an established career, and two younger ones recruited from India."

"That's unusual, I'd think. The forty-year-old lawyer, I mean."

"Apparently not so much these days when girls fresh from high school are rarely encouraged to enter religious life."

"Do the nuns keep to themselves?"

"Pretty much, but they've become more moderate over the years," said Garth. "They even accept guests from time to time. They have one right now, a writer needing some quiet time."

The abbey was off by itself in a wooded area near Black Springs, site of North America's first oil well. On the outskirts of the village, the cruiser turned off the highway onto a side road and slowed at the nearly-hidden entrance to a heavily treed property. A laneway twisted through tangled bush before passing between stone gateposts and ending in a cobblestone parking lot.

Now in plain view, Black Springs Abbey loomed before them, a neglected neo-gothic structure. Ivy wrapped itself protectively around the building's pale yellow brick exterior, creeping across windows and partially obscuring ornate brackets under the roof's projecting eaves. Third-storey dormer windows gazed blankly from the once-elegant mansard roof, slate tiles now faded and chipped. Wide stone steps, worn and cracked, led up to a double oak door with a rectangular transom window.

"Creepy," breathed Hilma. "Why would a guest want to stay here?"

"Peace and security, I suppose."

Hilma couldn't imagine finding either in a place like this but kept the thought to herself.

Stepping from the vehicle, she followed Garth around the side of the abbey to a thick wooden gate set into a high stone wall. He tugged at a rope attached to an iron bell atop the wall and soon they heard the sound of approaching steps. With a squeak, a peep hole opened in the gate's grille.

"It's Garth Mayfield," said the police constable.

Following the click of bolts, the gate swung open on creaky hinges.

"Nice to see you again, Garth," said an elderly woman, admitting the visitors into an overgrown garden enclosed in a crumbling stone wall. She wore sandals and a blue chambray pinafore over a long tunic of the same colour.

"I see you've brought a friend," she added, appraising Hilma with her keen dark eyes.

"Sister Helen, I'd like you to meet Hilma Moonstorey," said Garth.

"Azur's sister," said the nun thoughtfully.

Yes, her weird runaway sister. Isn't that what you're thinking? thought Hilma. *And how is it you know Azur?*

"Sister Helen is the porter and herbalist," said Garth.

Without comment, the nun led them along a covered cloister walkway and through a back door into the abbey kitchen. They followed her slow steps past cupboards with high glass-fronted doors, shiny sinks and polished stoves. Copper pots and pans hung from hooks above a central preparation area. The scent of freshly baked bread hung in the air.

"This is Sister Colleen's domain," said their escort, nodding in the direction of a sprightly little woman wearing a hairnet over her grey curls.

"Just missed tea," the cook scolded in response to Garth's greeting.

"I'll come earlier next time," he promised.

Garth and Hilma trailed Sister Helen through narrow halls carpeted in faded runners until she stopped before a partly closed door. "You have visitors, Mother Abbess," she announced.

"Come in," came a voice from within.

They entered a room whose paneled walls were lined in leather-bound books, some in glass cases, others on open shelves.

The abbess sat before a computer which shared a huge antique desk with stacks of papers and periodicals. She smiled and gestured for them to be seated on nearby brocade wing chairs, the fabric faded and worn.

"You must be Azur's sister," she said when Garth introduced the young woman who accompanied him.

"How do you know Azur?" asked Hilma, recalling that the porter had made the same comment.

"Azur is our nurse practitioner. She's been attending to our health since our physician retired last year."

"Does she make house calls here?" asked Hilma in surprise.

"Indeed she does. Did you not know she came out here?"

"Azur is very proper when it comes to professional confidentiality," said Hilma, annoyed that her sister had not shared this information with her. There was a time when there were no secrets between them.

"Everything fine with you, Aunt Jane?" asked Garth.

"I'm keeping well considering my age," said the abbess. "How are your parents?"

"They seem to be enjoying life in Arizona. I don't hear from them all that much."

"They always liked to gallivant," said the abbess.

Having spent most of his childhood in boarding schools while his parents attended to international business matters, her great-nephew murmured in agreement.

"Garth, I called you here today because I hoped you'd be able to recommend someone reliable to give us a hand now that Claude's gone," said the abbess.

"Claude was their custodian and groundskeeper," explained Garth to Hilma.

"His arthritis had gotten so bad that we found a retirement home placement for him," said the abbess. "He was very reluctant to move."

"It will be difficult to find another jack-of-all-trades," said Garth.

"Actually, with just the seven of us here, our needs have been changing. I'd like to hire someone who could assist more with shopping and errands. Maybe take on some management responsibilities in time."

"There's a job for you," Garth said teasingly to Hilma.

"Are you looking for work, Hilma?" asked the abbess, brightening.

"I think my grandparents would prefer I do something with my music," she said hastily.

"Oh, my dear, you haven't met Sister Beatrice!" said Mother Abbess. "She's a gifted organist and liturgist."

"My instruments are cello and harp," said Hilma.

"You'd make a wonderful team then," said the abbess undeterred.

Hilma sent a pleading look to Garth but the abbess smoothly intercepted his focus.

"Garth, since you're being kept from work," she suggested, "why don't you leave Hilma here for lunch with us, and come back for her in an hour or two!"

"Is that okay with you, Hilma?" asked Garth warily.

Not knowing how to gracefully extract herself from the situation, Hilma accepted the invitation.

"I'll let your grandparents know where you are," said Garth on his way out the door.

"And I'll have Sister Colleen set an extra place at table," said the abbess, picking up her phone.

Two

"There's time for a brief tour of the abbey before lunch," said the abbess rising from her desk. "We'll start in the front hall."

Once more Hilma found herself following a nun through panelled halls, this time without Garth's reassuring presence.

As in most of the abbey, the floors of the two-storey high entrance hall were of wide oak planks, worn but painstakingly polished. Hilma recognized that she was on the other side of the heavy front doors she had noticed on her arrival. From this perspective, however, sunlight illuminated the door's stain glass transom window in vibrant jewel colours.

Hilma's gaze moved from the lovely window to a magnificent oak staircase winding upward out of sight.

"Our sleeping quarters are on the floor above," said the abbess. "There are seventy cells on the second floor and fifty on the third. Of course we only use a few of them now."

"Cells?" wondered Hilma aloud.

The abbess laughed. "That's what we call our little rooms," she explained.

"Like rooms in a college dorm," said Hilma.

The abbess nodded.

"There must have been a lot of people living here once," said Hilma.

"At one time, there were a hundred sisters, including postulants and novices, and there were always between twenty and thirty girls."

"Oh, it was a boarding school."

"It was a home for unwed mothers," replied the abbess.

"Really! Did the townspeople know?"

"A few of them did. But in those days, families went to great lengths to keep their daughters' *delicate* conditions secret."

"How long did the girls stay here?"

"Most of them were here for about a year and a half. Their parents brought them here as soon as they learned of the pregnancy and they remained for a year after the delivery to continue their training."

"They were taught child care," said Hilma approvingly.

"Oh no, dear," said the abbess. "The babies were adopted out within days of their births."

"So what training did the girls get?"

"I know it sounds archaic now, but unwed mothers were called penitents in those days to encourage them to develop spiritually. They worked alongside our postulants and novices inside the abbey as well as outside in the gardens and barns."

"I don't suppose the... penitents were paid," said Hilma.

The abbess looked at her in surprise. "Of course not," she said. "They were reimbursing the abbey for room, board and maternity care, all the while learning a variety of practical skills to prepare them for marriageable futures."

"And the families went along with this?"

"Why yes. Families welcomed the rehabilitation of their errant daughters. Wealthier families made generous donations to the abbey when they came back to pick them up. Some paid to have their girls attend classes with the postulants and earn a *Marywood Collegiate and Finishing School* diploma while they were here."

"I guess a certificate would justify their absence to the neighbours when they returned home."

"Undoubtedly," said the abbess.

"Did *nobody* bring their daughters home without the... rehab?"

"There were a few families who paid for their daughters' expenses upfront and brought them home immediately after the deliveries. A few even claimed the babies, pretending the grandmother or another relative had given birth. But this was rare."

Hilma could think of nothing to say.

Relieved that the outspoken young woman seemed satisfied, the abbess proceeded to escort her through other rooms and alcoves. Throughout the abbey, antique furnishings, vases, statues and paintings were tastefully displayed. Nonetheless, when they arrived at the parlour with its cozy fireplace, comfortable armchairs, and book-lined walls, Hilma was pleased to see a room that appeared lived-in.

It was then she heard organ music floating through the abbey halls, a Bach cantata being brilliantly played. The abbess did not miss the light in the girl's eyes. *Perfect timing*, she thought.

"Shall we go to the chapel and meet Sister Beatrice?" she asked.

Within the chapel, sun filtering through stain glass windows cast ribbons of colour across the marble holy water font and over the ornate pews lining the nave. Attractive mosaic patterns flowed around the walls of the apse behind the altar and tabernacle. A faint scent of candle wax and incense drifted through the air. But it was the magnificent pipe organ donated years earlier by a grateful benefactor that held the attention of the visitor.

The organist, a tall thin nun with wiry white hair, stopped playing and looked questioningly at the abbess.

"Sister Beatrice, this is Hilma Moonstorey, Azur's sister and a student of music," said the abbess.

"Pleased to meet you," said the organist without looking especially pleased.

"Hilma plays cello and harp," said the abbess. "There must be wonderful ensemble music written for either of those instruments with organ."

"Indeed, Mother Abbess," responded the organist.

"We can discuss this over lunch," said the abbess casually as she led Hilma away.

Adjacent to the kitchen, the refectory had long tables along two walls, still there from former times when nuns ate at one table while postulants, novices and penitents shared the other.

The space between the tables had been open in those days to allow servers to move about, but now a smaller table covered with white linen had been placed in this area. Hilma noticed that it had been set for five with dishes, cutlery, butter and a pitcher of ice water.

A chime rang melodiously and the porter and organist entered the refectory to join the abbess and their guest. Moments later, Sister Colleen emerged from the kitchen pushing a serving cart bearing a tureen of steaming clam chowder, a large bowl of salad and a basket heaped with thick slabs of the fresh bread Hilma had smelled earlier. The cook transferred her tempting offerings to one of the long tables.

Hilma bowed her head as the nuns recited a blessing in unison. She imitated them in serving herself from the long table and found the women surprisingly conversational.

"I'm hoping to persuade Hilma to look after supplies and errands for us, so I've been showing her around the abbey," the abbess said once they were all seated. "She could help you in the garden too, Sister Helen, when she isn't busy elsewhere."

Hilma took a sip of water to hide her uneasiness.

"There are several areas she hasn't yet seen," said the abbess. "I don't know if Garth's schedule will allow us time for them or not."

"What hasn't she seen, Mother Abbess?" asked Sister Colleen.

"The upper two floors. The sheds, garage and barns. The cemetery. The oil wells."

"It was all so lively once," said Sister Helen with a sigh.

"Perhaps Hilma would like to know what roles we previously had and how we divide tasks now," suggested the abbess.

"How far do you want us to go back?" asked Sister Beatrice.

"To the beginning."

"My goodness! The four of us were in our early teens. I'd been here three years when Helen arrived. Then two years later, Colleen came along with you, Jane."

Hilma noticed that they had dropped titles and were addressing each other informally. "So you attended high school here," she said.

"The equivalent," said the abbess. "Heavy on theology, though. Our teachers included the novice mistress who watched our every move from morning to night."

"Who'd have thought in those days that you'd become novice mistress yourself," mused the porter.

"I held that position for many years until they elected me to my present position," agreed the abbess. "In our present simplified lifestyle, I also pitch in with other tasks when necessary."

"Before I became housekeeper and cook, I was house mother to the penitents," contributed Sister Colleen. "Oh! Perhaps Hilma doesn't know about… the penitents," she said, casting an anxious glance at the abbess.

"She knows all about them," replied the abbess dryly. "Hilma has an inquisitive mind."

The visitor smiled vaguely.

"I guess it's my turn," said Sister Beatrice. "I've been organist and choir director forever, and I still arrange liturgy services, though on a far smaller scale."

"Beatrice had the voice of an angel so they sent her to Toronto to study with the best musicians," said the abbess. "Her knowledge includes keyboard, voice, theory, Gregorian chant and archival expertise."

At the praise, the organist's mouth softened into a slight smile. "For years we had the most beautiful choir," she said, the smile quickly fading.

"I've been porter and herbalist for ages," said Sister Helen when everyone turned their attention on her. "I still answer the door and tend the garden."

"Garth told me there were seven sisters," said Hilma, wondering where the three missing residents were.

"Sister Martha, our lawyer, is in family court today," said the abbess. "Family law is her specialty. And our two novices are upstairs practicing the art of journaling with Eula."

"Eula is a writer spending some time here as a guest," Sister Helen explained for Hilma's benefit.

"I suppose they're having lunch up there," said the organist, her voice tinged with disapproval.

The abbess nodded and sipped her tea.

"It's not good to spoil novices," continued Sister Beatrice. "I suppose you served them too, Colleen?"

"I sent their food up in the dumb waiter," said the cook.

"That's exactly what I mean," said Sister Beatrice. "They should have come down to the kitchen and prepared their own food. Granted Eula is a paying guest, but as for the other two, there was a time when novices earned their keep."

"The novices have lots of responsibilities," said the abbess mildly. "Along with their studies, they do all our laundry and mending and look after the chickens."

"And they've learned to drive the tractor and lawn mower now that Claude's gone," added Sister Helen, earning herself a glare from the organist.

"Are you in the healing arts like Azur and your grandmother?" asked Sister Colleen in an attempt to divert the conversation to a more agreeable subject.

"I'm afraid not," said Hilma.

"Hilma is a musician," said the abbess. "Tell the sisters about your accomplishments."

"Well," stammered the girl, "I play harp and cello."

"With a degree in what?" prompted the abbess.

"The physics of musical sound."

"Where do you intend to go with that?" asked Sister Beatrice.

"Hilma is in the early stages of her career," said the abbess when the young woman seemed at a loss for words. "Whatever else she does in life, music will always bring her joy."

She paused before adding, "I expect some lessons at the organ would enrich her background further." She looked pointedly at the organist who seemed about to speak, then lowered her eyes under the abbess's steely gaze.

"Hilma, let's slip upstairs and meet our novices and Eula before Garth returns for you," said the abbess.

"She hasn't had dessert yet," protested Sister Colleen. "I've made rice pudding."

"We'll have dessert with Garth," said the abbess. "The rest of you go ahead and finish."

"Shall I have Garth wait in the parlour?" asked the porter.

"Invite him for lunch if he hasn't eaten," instructed the abbess.

"This place is becoming more and more like an inn," muttered Sister Beatrice.

"Abbeys have traditionally provided hospitality to travellers," commented Sister Colleen, ignoring the organist's snort.

I would never take organ lessons from that miserable nun, thought Hilma as she followed the abbess from the refectory.

Three

"We'll take the back way to the second floor," said the abbess leading the way through the kitchen.

As they climbed the narrow stairs, she said over her shoulder, "You mustn't mind Sister Beatrice. She's really a decent soul."

One storey up, the stairs paused at a small landing before continuing to a third-floor. Glancing upward, Hilma noticed a girl with long brown hair gazing solemnly down at her from the third-floor landing.

Momentarily distracted, Hilma failed to notice that the abbess was holding the second-floor door open, waiting for her to enter.

"Hilma?" prompted the abbess gently.

"Sorry, Mother Abbess," murmured Hilma, reaching to take the door.

"You can call me Abbess," said the nun. "Only the sisters need call me Mother."

Hilma nodded.

"Right now we're at the west end of the abbey," explained the abbess. "The plumbing and electrical wiring have been updated in this area. Our rooms are along the west wall overlooking the cloister garden. We've merged cells so that each of our units has a washroom and bed-sitting area. It's quite a luxury for us!"

The abbess didn't offer to display any of the rooms' interiors.

"Here's our infirmary," she said, opening the door to a room on the northwest corner. Painted pale blue, the room contained an examining table, medical supply cupboards and a cot. A crucifix hung on the wall near the window.

"We'll go across to the south side and meet our novices and writer-in-residence," she said leading back past the sisters' rooms to the opposite hall. "We've modernized six units here as well."

They could hear voices and quiet laughter coming through the doorway of the fourth unit from the end. At the abbess' knock, the door was opened by a plumpish woman in her late thirties with a mass of thick brown curls. She was wearing a long brown skirt, an aqua sweater and black satin slippers.

"I've brought a visitor to meet you and our novices. May we come in?"

"By all means, Abbess," said the woman, stepping back from the door to allow them to enter. "We're just having our lunch break."

At their arrival, two young women with medium-length black hair rose quickly to their feet. They had sandaled feet and their habits consisted of a white pinafore over a navy tunic.

"Mother Abbess," they murmured in unison.

"Hilma Moonstorey is a talented musician," the abbess told them. "She's Azur Moonstorey-Barkley's sister."

The threesome greeted her warmly and introduced themselves.

"Eula Jennings," said the woman in slippers. "I'm a bit of a recluse and this is the ideal place for me to write mysteries in peace and quiet while being totally spoiled by the sisters."

"I'm Sister Fazeela. I like it here too although I miss my family back home in India a bit." She smiled apologetically at the abbess.

The abbess reached out and touched the young woman's arm sympathetically.

"My name is Sister Jamini," said the other novice. "I'm very happy at the abbey."

"Hilma may help us with ordering supplies and running errands into town."

"That would be lovely, Hilma," said Eula. "You could bring me books from the Black Springs library. I hate to keep bothering Sister Martha when she's so busy."

Hilma thought it odd that a writer wouldn't want to access the library herself.

"Will you be living here?" asked Sister Jamini.

Before Hilma could reply, the abbess interjected. "If you decide to join us, Hilma, you could have the room next to Eula's. It's been modernized and never used. Let's go have a peek."

She walked quickly to the adjacent room, trailed by the others. The unit had beige walls with white-trimmed baseboards and windows. As in every abbey room, a crucifix hung on the wall.

No room for the devil here, thought Hilma. An image of the psychic vampire, Vek, sprang unbidden to her mind and she shook it off.

"Once you bring your own things, it will be cozy and friendly," said Eula.

"And look, you'd have your own bathroom," said Sister Fazeela.

Feeling overwhelmed, Hilma feared the onset of a panic attack. Recognizing her discomfort, the abbess smoothly deflected the issue, commenting that Hilma needed time to think things over.

When the abbess and her visitor exited onto the backstairs, Hilma noticed that the girl she had seen previously no longer stood on the upper landing. She asked the abbess if anyone lived up there.

"The third floor has been vacant for many years and is just used for storage," said the abbess.

On the way down, the abbess mentioned that Garth might have arrived by now. Hilma fervently hoped so. However, when they reached the refectory, the sisters were at the table sipping tea and Garth was nowhere in sight.

"I haven't served the rice pudding yet because I wanted it to stay warm," said Sister Colleen, rising. "I'll go get it." She bustled off towards the kitchen pushing the cart now stacked with dirty dishes.

The abbess and Hilma took the places they had vacated for their upstairs visit. The guest felt the sisters' eyes upon her as she fidgeted with her napkin.

"Did you meet Eula and Sisters Fazeela and Jamini?" asked Sister Beatrice. She seemed more subdued and Hilma wondered if the other sisters had admonished her for the disparaging remarks she had made in front of a visitor.

Hilma assured the organist that she had met all three.

"Does your grandmother still harvest herbs?" Sister Helen asked her.

"Yes, she does," said Hilma, surprised that the porter would know this.

"Your grandmother's kindness and talents are well known," said the abbess. "As a young midwife, she delivered many of our babies."

Really? Mavis delivered abbey babies? What else don't I know about my family? wondered Hilma.

When Sister Colleen returned with her replenished serving cart, those seated at the table rose and followed her to the long table, waiting as she set out a bowl of rice pudding generously dotted with raisins, a small pitcher of cream, a cinnamon shaker and a stack of small dessert bowls. One by one they spooned pudding into little bowls, added cream and cinnamon and returned to their places.

"There was a time when we were self-sufficient," said the cook. "We raised our own food and had essential supplies delivered."

"We had a goat herd and horses but now we only have a few chickens and whatever will grow in the garden," added Sister Helen wistfully.

"This pudding is delicious," said Hilma. "So was everything else."

"Thank you," said the cook. "It really would be nice if you came to help us, and I'm not saying that just because you complimented the food."

The nuns looked at the young woman expectantly. At that moment, the back doorbell rang, saving her from further scrutiny.

"That will be Garth," said the abbess. "Please bring him in for lunch. He probably hasn't taken time to eat."

Sister Colleen rose to collect another place setting while Sister Helen excused herself and soon returned with the police constable. He readily accepted the lunch invitation and helped himself to the food set out on the long table.

"How did you know I hadn't eaten?" he asked, laughing as he joined them at table.

"I figured you wouldn't leave our guest longer than necessary," said the abbess.

"Hilma may be willing to work here," she said as soon as her great-nephew was seated.

"That would be great," said Garth.

"I'm still thinking about it," said Hilma, concealing the rising anger she felt over the presumptuousness of the company in which she found herself.

"Take all the time you need," said the abbess reassuringly. "Maybe you can start with a couple of days a week while still living at home."

"Could I accept the position and continue to live at home?" asked Hilma.

"Well, you *could*," said the abbess. "But living here would give you more time for music and leisure. You can keep your harp and cello in the cell next to your room."

"You could still go home when you felt the need," said Sister Helen.

"I'll discuss it with my grandparents," said Hilma evasively.

Four

Hilma was annoyed at how readily Mavis and Bram took to the idea of their younger granddaughter working at the abbey.

"Surely you don't approve of me *living* there!" she said indignantly as they relaxed in the sitting room the following afternoon sipping herbal tea.

"It would be no different than being away at college," said Bram.

"Except for the work part and the fact that the only ones my age are two novices," said Hilma.

"Think of it as a co-op placement," said Bram.

"A co-op placement behind bars," she retorted sullenly.

"Why don't you visit the abbey again, and this time take Azur with you?" suggested Mavis. "It'll give you another opportunity to assess how you feel about the place."

As if on cue, the front door opened and Azur's voice called out cheerfully, "Company calling!"

The older granddaughter entered the room in the company of her husband, Dr. Xavier Tennyson Barkley, and police constable, Garth Mayfield. Hilma and her grandparents looked up in surprise.

"Quiet day at the clinic and police station?" asked Mavis.

"Others in the team are covering for us," said Xavier Tennyson.

"The babies aren't coming early!" said Bram, concern in his voice.

"The babies have no intention of appearing for two months, Bram," said Azur. "Relax!"

"We wanted to let you know that we're going with Garth to meet the abbess," explained XT to his in-laws.

"I'm not ready to go!" said Hilma, jumping to her feet and spilling tea on her jeans.

"Maybe it's not about you for once," said Azur.

"Now girls," interjected Bram.

"Garth contacted XT to see if he'd be interested in investing in a condo housing project," said Azur. "We're both quite intrigued with the idea."

"How does the abbess come into this?" asked Bram.

"The condos would be at the abbey," said Garth.

"At the abbey!" exclaimed Hilma. "When did all this happen?"

"After I dropped you off yesterday, I got a phone call at the police station from Aunt Jane saying she had something else to run by me," said Garth. "I went out after work and she told me that for some time the sisters have been tossing about revenue ideas such as retreat rooms on the second floor and condos on the third. They're looking for investment partners."

"So Garth called me to see if I would be interested in joining him in the venture," said XT.

"Bram and Mavis thought the abbey would make a wonderful co-op placement for me," said Hilma facetiously.

"Yes, Garth told us about the possibility of organ lessons combined with some work for the nuns," said XT, ignoring his sister-in-law's sarcasm. "I hope you're considering it."

"It's a wonderful opportunity," said Azur to her sister.

"I think the condo idea is a much better plan," said Hilma. "Perhaps it'll keep all your underworked minds from fussing over me."

"There's no reason why both undertakings couldn't happen simultaneously," said Garth, trying to hide his disappointment at her dismissive attitude.

"We stopped by here because we thought you'd be reassured by the idea of us being involved with the abbey while you're there," said XT. "That is, if you decide to go," he added hastily.

"Why don't you come with us now, Hilma, while we talk to the abbess about her investment ideas," urged Azur. "You might think of some questions that don't occur to us."

"The abbess will think I've come to stay," said her sister with rising anxiety.

"We'll make it clear that we're strictly there on business," Garth assured her.

★ ★ ★

A half hour later, Hilma participated in her second abbey tour of the week. This time, she was able to wander at a slower pace through kitchen, chapel, refectory, library and parlour in the company of Garth, Azur and XT. The four were also shown the laundry, conference room and other nooks and crannies. Then the abbess led them up the curving front staircase to the upper floor.

"I haven't come this way before," said Azur, stopping to admire the ornate oak banister.

"No, you've always come up the back stairs to the infirmary and the rooms we currently use," said the abbess.

The staircase led to a wide second-floor landing with tall double doors on either side.

"The northern side has always been the sisters' residence," explained the abbess, leading them through doors on the right. "The other side was where novices and the expectant mothers lived in our busier days."

Their footsteps echoed hollowly as they followed the abbess along the north hall. As they walked, she explained that the long hallway separated cells along the exterior windowed side from shared washrooms and service rooms on the interior side.

"This is a typical cell," she said stepping inside a small room containing a cot with bare mattress, a bedside table, a desk with chair, an open closet with a deep drawer beneath it and a sink with a metal towel rack. There was a small lamp on the desk and one on the table. A small window above the desk overlooked the cloister garden.

"Of course, the cells would have been cosier when they had towels, bedding, curtains and personal belongings," suggested Azur.

"And more personal," agreed the abbess.

"How many cells all together?" asked XT.

"One hundred and twenty. Seventy on this floor and fifty on the floor above."

"You said the sisters, novices and pregnant girls were on this floor," noted Azur. "Who lived on the third floor?"

"Postulants and young women who had already given birth."

"The penitents," mumbled Hilma.

The abbess regarded her thoughtfully. "We are all penitents," she said gently.

Abashed, Hilma nodded mutely.

"Perhaps you're wondering what postulants are," continued the abbess. "They're young women in their first year of discernment. At the end of the year, they take their First Vows and become novices. Hilma has already met our two novices."

She gave Hilma a comradely smile as they continued down the hall. Hilma moved closer to Garth.

"Here's where Sister Helen currently dries her herbs and garlic," she said, opening another door to reveal rows of hanging plants in varying stages of dehydration. "And here's the infirmary where Azur visits us from time to time." She and Azur exchanged warm smiles.

At the end of the hall, she pointed out an exit door and a connecting corridor with cells overlooking the cloister garden. "These are our rooms," she said. "The opposite hall is a mirror image of the one you've just seen with the exception of some recently renovated units."

She led them through the exit door and up the back stairs to the unused third floor where dust and cobwebs flourished. Hilma looked about cautiously for the mystery girl but could find no evidence that anyone had been there.

"The dormer windows are a lovely feature," noted Azur, standing in the doorway of a tiny cell.

"Lots of potential for condos up here," agreed XT.

The group descended the back stairs to the kitchen and from there followed the abbess into the walled cloister garden. An arched opening in the back stone partition led to a walled cemetery. Simple white crosses with the names of deceased nuns and the dates of their lifespans surrounded a marble statue of the Holy Family. They retraced their steps through the cloister garden and thence through the gate to the outside property.

"From here you can see the sheds, garage and barns," said the abbess. "The entire twenty acres is fringed with evergreens, providing privacy as well as protection from the elements. We once had a dairy goat herd. Now we just have a few chickens. And the oil wells."

"Who looks after the wells?" asked XT.

"They require very little maintenance. The oil is piped to the road and every few weeks a truck comes around and collects it. There used to be fifteen active wells but now we're down to six."

"What happened to the others?" asked Azur.

"Over time, they became unproductive and were shut down."

"It's all very interesting, Abbess" said XT. "You've been very gracious, thank you."

"Shall we go sit inside?" she asked invitingly.

They followed the abbess back through the cloister garden and into the abbey parlour where they sank gratefully into armchairs arranged in an intimate semicircle facing the fireplace. The abbess insisted that Azur sit with her feet elevated on an ottoman.

"What are your thoughts at this time?" she asked them.

"It's a beautiful place," said XT. "Of course, it would need rewiring and plumbing."

"It needs a lot of work including re-roofing," added the abbess.

"It needs an elevator," said Azur wearily.

"Perhaps you shouldn't have climbed all those stairs," said the abbess. "The thought occurred to me at the time, but I figured that you, of all people, would practice common sense."

"I know my limits," Azur assured her. "It was good exercise."

"You're right, though," said XT to his wife. "An elevator will have to be a priority."

"We'll have to hire an architect to guide us through the process," said Garth.

"What do you ladies think – apart from the elevator?" asked XT.

"I love the place!" said Azur fervently. "It has such a warm, embracing atmosphere. Don't you feel it, Hilma?"

Hilma remained silent for several moments. "It's hard to explain," she admitted finally, "but it does feel welcoming." She glanced hesitantly at Garth and he smiled warmly in return.

"Might you be interested then in becoming investment partners with us?" asked the abbess.

"It goes without saying that I'm in," said Garth.

XT looked at his wife who gave him a fervent nod.

"We're honoured that you've invited us to join you, Abbess," he said.

"Would you consider including another couple if we vouched for them? asked Azur.

Five

Hilma was playing harp arpeggios in the upstairs music room of the home she shared with her grandparents when the upper hall telephone began ringing persistently. Bram and Mavis were downtown shopping so, sighing, she went to answer it.

"Hilma? Is that you?" The voice sounded vaguely familiar but Hilma couldn't quite place it.

"Yes," she replied tentatively.

"It's Eula. From the abbey?"

"Oh, yes," said Hilma cautiously.

"I was wondering if you were free this morning to take a drive around Black Springs with me. Garth has agreed to drive us."

The suggestion caught Hilma off guard.

"Hilma? Are you there?"

"Did the abbess put you up to this? Or was it Garth?" Despite being suspicious in an annoyed sort of way, her heart fluttered at the mention of his name.

"It was entirely my idea," insisted Eula. "I've never spent any time in Black Springs and I keep hearing how pleasant and inviting the village is, and I thought since you might be doing errands and shopping for the abbey, somebody would be showing you around, and it would be the ideal time for me to tag along, and..."

Hilma interrupted the woman's rambling. "What's the main reason?"

"Okay, when the abbess introduced us, I recognized you as a person trying to find your way. A person like me. And I wanted you to have the same chance at finding peace and contentment that I've had at the abbey."

"I see."

"But, Hilma, I really am welcoming an opportunity to browse around Black Springs. It's the writer in me."

"The browsing won't take long," said Hilma dryly.

Eula chuckled. "I guess that's why Garth suggested we also visit the museum and the Fairbank oilfields."

"What happened to Eula the recluse?"

"I'm not a recluse by choice. But that's a story for another day."

"Okay. Just don't tell the abbess I'm ripe for hiring."

"I won't, but I'm going to call Garth now to pick you up."

No sooner had Hilma freshened up and put on her jacket when Garth announced himself with a brisk knock at the front door. In his usual obliging fashion, he opened the cruiser passenger door for her.

"Are you on duty?" she asked.

"Sure," he said. "Accompanying ladies in the safety of my vehicle is all in a day's work."

"This doesn't mean I'm committed to your master plan," she said, clicking into her seatbelt.

"There is no master plan."

"How do you know Eula?"

"I met her briefly when she stopped into the police station a few months back and asked for help finding a safe secluded place. After I ran her name through the system and was satisfied that she was respectable, I phoned Aunt Jane who told me to bring her right over."

"Was she running from something?"

"Her marriage, but she chose not to elaborate."

"What has she been told about me?" she asked suspiciously.

"Nothing, as far as I know."

They drove in silence to the abbey, Garth sensing her need to settle into a calm centre. Eula was waiting at the cloister gate wearing sunglasses, black slacks and a beige sweater. A large black beret was pulled over her curly hair. After Garth helped her into the back seat, they drove towards the village.

"Can anyone see me in here?" asked Eula.

"Not readily. The windows are tinted as well as barred," he said.

"Besides you're well-disguised," said Hilma, inwardly rolling her eyes.

"Are the doors locked?"

"Always," said Garth.

Hilma realized that the writer truly was as anxious and insecure as she was. It was sobering to know that the woman was venturing out into perceived danger to try to help her.

"There won't be many people where we're going," she reassured her.

"It only takes one," said Eula.

When they reached the west end of the village's business section, Garth noted that there used to be hotels, service centres and an open-air dance pavillion at this intersection with Barnes Hotel on the north side of the road and Oxford House on the south.

"They're long gone, of course," he said, "but there *is* a beautiful golf course down the road to the west. We'll save it for another day."

"How nice that there's a restaurant, convenience store, LCBO and U Haul rentals here now," noted Eula brightly, taking in the corner complex.

"It must be a relief for the people who live here to have wine and spirits close at hand," muttered Hilma.

As they neared the village centre, Garth told them that the streets had once been lined with thriving businesses: a shoe store, a harness shop, Sherman House, Cameron House,

Duffy Apartments, garages, shoe and harness repair shops and a millinery shop.

"Lots of *used-to-bes*," said Hilma.

"Think of the rich history," said Eula.

"Here are some *active* businesses," said Garth pointedly. He slowed before a TV and satellite store occupying the building of a former hardware store and lumber yard, and pointed out an insurance office in the old Hydro building.

"Did you notice the lovely cenotaph and the nicely-landscaped warehouse?" asked Eula.

"The warehouse guys specialize in basement repairs and renovations," explained Garth.

"Does the place have a train station?" asked Hilma.

Garth looked at her warily.

"Just curious," she said defensively.

"Actually, the tracks ran right through here between Margaret Street and where that fire station is," said Garth. "I'll show you where the train station was in a few minutes."

He told them that the fire station they were passing occupied the site of a once-upon-a-time meat market and was across from another garage.

"It must have been a vibrant place," said Eula, her writer's imagination transporting her back in time.

"More than four thousand people at its peak," said Garth. "On our right is the Municipal Office on the site of the Dewar building which housed a drug store, bank and apartments.

"Council chambers in there?" asked Hilma, deciding to show a bit of appreciation for their efforts.

"Yes, and the clerk's office."

"Oh, look, Hilma," said Eula. "The post office and library are in that lovely red brick building. How long has it been there, Garth?"

"Since 1932 when it was built to replace the wooden frame Town Hall and Cape's General Store which burnt down the same day. There used to be a bakery and grocery store beside the post office and next to that another general store. Across the road was another general store, flour and feed business and a grocery."

"Imagine people crowding the stores shopping and going about their business," said Eula.

"Horses with carriages, vendors and inns," added Garth.

"Imagine painted ladies, bar brawls, board walks, clay roads, and women holding up their skirts to minimize the mud splashing on their hems and boots," said Hilma, recalling the brief time she'd spent in Prosper Station before the irrationality of Vapourlea almost stole her soul.

"You seem quite knowledgeable about Victorian times," said Eula.

"Only some aspects of it."

"We're turning onto Kelly Road," said Garth, veering to the right. "On the southeast corner are the Oddfellows building and village variety. Most recently there's been a café there and a place to pick up wheelchairs."

"Looks kinda vacant now," noted Hilma.

"What a grand old building!" exclaimed Eula. "I hope they preserve it and find a good use for it."

"We're passing the former sites of the Little White Brick Post Office and a doctor's office," said the police guide.

"Where?" queried Hilma sardonically as she surveyed overgrown, vacant lots.

Disregarding the apathy of his front-seat passenger, Garth carried on. "At the intersection ahead is Watson's Machine Shop and the old blacksmith's shop. Murray Watson worked there until recently. You'll see his metal sculptures along the route we'll be taking."

He made a right turn on Victoria Street and, as they drove past more weedy fields, he recited the names of former businesses that once existed here: Dominion Boiler, Winnet Apartments, a coal and lumber yard. Without even trying to make a point, Hilma yawned. Garth clenched his jaw, clearly piqued by her childish behaviour.

"Sorry," she said.

"For what?"

"For seeming unappreciative," she admitted.

Garth gave her hand a forgiving squeeze and she smiled back contritely.

"Tada!" he said, bringing the cruiser to a halt after turning right onto Margaret Street.

"What?" chorused his passengers.

"This is where the train depot was."

"On a parking lot across from a laundromat and carwash?" Hilma felt unreasonably disappointed.

"Yes. They moved it to the Canadian Oil Museum in 1960 after it was no longer in service. We'll take a peek at it on our way to the oil fields."

"The village should have descriptive plaques with photos placed at significant spots," said Eula.

"They do have a few," said Garth, "but such things take money."

Garth continued west on Victoria Street, pointing out a large community centre and an impressive ball diamond, then drove south on the highway and east on Gum Bed Line.

"We're now on our way to visit two designated National Historic Sites," he said.

"Here?" asked Hilma in disbelief.

"Yes. The Oil Museum of Canada and the Fairbank oilfields."

"The museum is remarkable," he said as he circled the driveway around the front of the building. "James Miller Williams dug an oil well on this site in 1858 and created North America's first commercial oil business. The museum has four climate controlled indoor galleries and seven outdoor interpretive buildings. Visitors are always pleasantly surprised."

"There should be throngs of people here!" exclaimed Eula. "Though I'm glad they're not here today," she added with a shiver.

"We don't have time to get out," said Garth, "but there's your train station, Hilma." He pointed to a charmingly restored board and batten building at the front of the museum property.

"You have an interest in train stations?" Eula asked her.

"More like a horror fascination," she said.

"Before I take you ladies home, we'll do a sweep around the oilfields.

"This village badly needs a PR person," noted Hilma.

"Are you volunteering?"

"I'm not the publicity type," she snorted. "Besides certain people seem to already have plans for me."

Her comment went unchallenged.

"Now, ladies, you're about to see an oilfield still working efficiently on nineteenth-century technology," announced Garth.

He went on to relate how Charlie Fairbank was insistent on maintaining an oilfield compatible with nature. Throughout his property were trails, wildflowers, wildlife and domestic sheep to keep the grass cropped. Two llamas protected the sheep from coyotes and, although Charlie hired shearers for the wool, he raised the sheep himself down to overseeing the complexities of lambing.

Along Gum Bed Line, Garth slowed at significant places animated by Murray Watson's metal sculptures. At the oil receiving station, a team of life-size metal horses hitched to a wagon bearing a wooden tank of crude oil waited while two historical figures supervised the unloading process. Further along the road, another iron horse team was on its way to the receiving station.

They passed a pioneer pump block, its horizontal beam slowly teeter-tottering as it pumped oil flowing through a pipe to a collecting tank. Not far away, the James Rig, one of six powerhouses on the property, operated on a five-horsepower motor which replaced steam in 1918. Garth explained how a field wheel horizontally shifted the jerker line system in various directions.

"The jerker line system was devised in 1863 by Charlie Fairbank's great grandfather, John Henry," said Garth. "It connects several wells, allowing them to share a central power source."

East of the powerhouse, he insisted they go on foot to see an underground wooden storage tank, a three-pole derrick and a pump kit wagon. The setting was livened by more of the whimsical sculptures along with a child-friendly *Thomas the Tank Engine* created from an oil tank.

In one metallic scenario, a likeness of Charlie's younger son sat on a pump kit wagon, the family dog at his side, a figure climbed a derrick while another held a wrench, a teamster tended his horses and a foreman stood atop an underground tank.

Off Gypsy Flat Road, Garth pointed out the location of wells in the woods, a 1940-model metal pump jack, and the Jury and Evoy flowing well which had required no pump to bring oil to the surface. Dug in 1862 to a depth of sixty feet, it produced 300 barrels a day, and when bored through to a deeper level, 2000 barrels poured forth daily until it petered out a year later.

Hilma's mind was wandering and she had to stifle the urge to yawn again. To distract herself, she visualized a musical score she was mastering for cello and imagined her bow humming across the instrument's strings.

"Look at the painting on that barn!" exclaimed Eula, bringing Hilma back to the moment. She looked over at a colourful mural of a man driving a team of horses pulling an oil wagon.

"Charlie's barn," said Garth. "It's an early logo of VanTuyl and Fairbank Hardware."

On their way back to the village centre, they passed two apartment complexes, one in a former schoolhouse, the other in the old creamery.

With the tour completed, Garth dropped Eula off at the abbey and drove Hilma home. She thanked him as she stepped from the cruiser, quickly averting her eyes from the affection she glimpsed in his.

Six

On a balmy morning in the first week of June, Azur drove Dillian Kilgour to see Black Springs Abbey for the first time. Her long-time friend had left her son, Gideon, age two, with his grandmother, Ethel Witherton, but Azur was accompanied by four-year-old Meredith who sat in the back seat of the Subaru Forester.

"I can't wait to see this abbey of yours," said Dilly.

"Today works out nicely because I'm working the evening shift in Emerg."

"They called me this morning to supply teach but I told them that I had another commitment," said Dilly.

"Do you enjoy supply teaching?"

"I don't really mind it though I'd much rather have my own art studio. I'm not as crazy about teaching as Graeme is, or for that matter, as you are in being a nurse practitioner."

"Who looks after Meri and Gideon when you work?" asked Azur.

"I have an accommodating neighbour who can usually take them on short notice. She used to run a day care and she still has all her books and toys."

"I'm so glad Graeme was able to get a transfer from Wickford to the Providence Crossing high school," said Azur.

"It will be wonderful moving back to the old home town," agreed her friend. "Mother said we can stay with her until we find a suitable house."

When the car came to a stop in front of Black Springs Abbey, Azur waited for her friend's reaction.

"It's awesome," said Dilly softly. "Such a romantic setting."

"You're not put off by the decrepit appearance?"

"That and the eeriness are all part of its allure."

The women helped Meri from the back seat of the car and walked around to the back of the abbey. The gate to the cloister garden was open and a man whose hair was liberally sprinkled with grey was speaking with Sister Helen.

"Come in," said the porter when she saw the women and the little girl, clutching a faded pink blanket. "I was expecting you."

"Good morning, Sister Helen," said Azur. "I'd like you to meet my friend, Dillian Kilgour and her daughter, Meredith, known by one and all as Meri. Dilly is a talented artist."

"Your daughter has been blessed with your lovely red hair and curls," observed the nun after they had exchanged greetings. Then she turned to the man.

"This is Claude Gronseth, our long-time gardener and caretaker," she said. "He's living in Providence Crossing now that he's retired."

"It's hard to stay away from the place," said Claude, reluctantly taking his leave after introductions to the women.

Sister Helen bolted the gate behind him and escorted the women and child into the abbey.

"Claude came to the abbey while I was still a novice," she told them. "He was only ten years old."

"Why so young?" asked Dilly.

"They were a very poor family. His father had died and his mother couldn't afford to feed her brood of children. She distributed them among relatives so that she could hire herself out as a domestic. When she couldn't find a place for Claude, she brought him here."

"And never came back?" asked Dilly.

"At first she visited regularly but the visits dwindled away after Sister Beatrice told her they were upsetting," said the nun.

"Upsetting to whom?" asked Azur.

"To Claude," said the porter. "Sister Beatrice had taken it upon herself to oversee his upbringing. He wasn't a keen student so when he showed a knack for fixing things, she steered him in that direction. Eventually he took over all the custodial and groundskeeping duties."

"Has he no interaction with his family?" asked Dilly.

"He lost contact with his siblings during his first years here," said the nun. "Later he had a wife but early in their marriage, she took their infant son and left. Claude went after them and managed to bring back the baby but he couldn't convince Lorraine to return with him. Broke his heart."

"What happened to the baby?" asked Dilly.

"Claude didn't seem to know what to do with an infant so Sister Beatrice found adoptive parents for him."

"So sad," sighed Dilly.

"If you would be so kind as to escort us to the front hall, Sister Helen, I'll take Dilly and Meri upstairs myself," said Azur.

The porter willingly complied, showing Dilly some of the highlights of the main floor as they walked through the abbey. Dillian was suitably impressed by the time-worn elegance of the building.

After wandering through rooms on the two upper floors, Azur and Dilly entered one of the second-floor cells and shut the door to confine the curious Meri. The women sat on the bare mattress and laughed about what it must have been like to live here when abbey life was at its prime.

"From what I've read about hospital schools of nursing, they weren't a whole lot different in those days," said Azur.

"Do you think often about our train ride back in time?" asked Dilly.

"I don't dwell on it, but it's hard to walk by the library or visit my family at Warren Avenue without having flashbacks of Prosper Station."

Dilly nodded empathetically. "How is Hilma doing?"

"I doubt that Hilma will ever be the carefree, confident girl she was before being in Vek's clutches," said Azur, shaking her head. "The first year back was hell for everyone, especially Bram and Mavis."

"Thank God your grandparents had XT to help her with withdrawal while you were away interning."

"And thank heavens Mavis is skilled in herbology and the healing arts," added Azur.

"Is it still worrisome for all of you as Hallowe'en approaches?"

"Hilma is never left alone the last two weeks of October. As Hallowe'en draws near, XT and I move in with them on Warren Avenue so we're always there overnight. Hilma seems relieved, you know, because she doesn't trust herself even now. She likens it to a vertigo experience where one feels irresistibly drawn to plunge from a summit."

"How horrible," said Dilly. "How are the music lessons going?"

"She quit."

"Oh, no! Why ever did she do that? She's so musically gifted," groaned Dilly.

"It's a long story," said Azur. "Things are looking brighter, though. She's been offered work here at the abbey, helping the sisters with shopping and errands. The details have yet to be sorted out but a bonus is that she'd be able to study music here with the organist, Sister Beatrice."

"That *is* encouraging. Is that why you and XT are investing in the abbey?"

Azur explained to her friend how the idea evolved from the nuns' search for revenue ideas to keep their beloved abbey open.

"Graeme and I really appreciate that you invited us to be partners," said Dilly.

"Do you think you'll come on board?" asked Azur.

"We're seriously considering it. Graeme wants to sit down with all the partners to talk about financing and legalities."

"It would be much more fun with us all involved," said Azur.

"I'm trying to imagine the logistics of renovating this magnificent building while still maintaining the ambience," said Dilly, walking over to the window.

"Beautiful, beautiful," she murmured, surveying the view. "I could see myself living here."

"Do you feel like that too?" asked Azur, rising laboriously to her feet after sitting so long.

"The last trimester of pregnancy can be trying," sympathized her friend.

"You survived it," laughed Azur, joining her friend at the window.

"Yes, but I wasn't carrying twins. Did I hear you say you'd like to live here?" asked Dilly, studying her friend reflectively.

"I would," replied Azur. "But I'm not sure how it would fit with the guys' investment plans."

"I would *love* to live here," said Dilly. "I could have the most beautiful studio in the world. I'd teach painting in every possible media… there'd be a pottery wheel and a kiln… you'd come home from the clinic to relax in your own paradise… and Hilma would play music when she wasn't helping the sisters."

Azur smiled at her friend's enthusiastic rambling. "It sounds idyllic," she said.

"It *would* be idyllic, Azur! Imagine raising children in this beautiful place!"

"Hilma would be more apt to stay if we were here," mused Azur.

"So you do agree," said Dilly hopefully.

"I'm thinking aloud," said Azur. "Dreams don't always translate into reality."

"But this one could," persisted Dilly. "We'd simply be living in abbey condos instead of in houses in town."

"Would you try to retain some of the abbey features in your condo?" asked Azur, interested in her friend's artistic instincts.

"Definitely."

"What would you do with all the little cells on the third floor?"

"It would take some creative planning, but I'm sure they could be combined in an aesthetically pleasing way."

"You realize, of course, that the men are visualizing the investment potential of the abbey," said Azur. "How do you think they'd take to the idea of living here?"

"That will also take some creative planning," said Dilly. "When are they getting together?"

"Saturday morning," said Azur.

"We'll be ready for them," said her friend with a conspiratorial grin.

Seven

Saturday morning provided a perfect June day to wander the grounds of Black Springs Abbey. Clematis, honeysuckle, climbing roses and assorted vines disguised sagging sheds and crumbling walls in drapes of nostalgic beauty. In the meadow, grasshopper-like pump jacks bowed and bobbed among the dancing wildflowers, butterflies and dragonflies. Birds chirped and called from nearby tree branches while insects buzzed and hummed in the vegetation below.

Garth Mayfield had invited Hilma to tag along while he, Graeme Kilgour and Dr. XT Barkley, inspected the property. It couldn't have worked out better for Hilma's undercover role on behalf of Azur and Dilly.

"Hey, guys! Look at this!" called XT, bending over something hidden in the tall grasses and waving blooms.

The other men walked over to look at XT's discovery.

"It's a holding tank filled with black oily stuff," said Graeme, lifting up one edge of an old wooden cover to peer beneath it.

"The tanks on the Fairbank property are much larger than this," Hilma informed them.

"Hilma has become an authority on the oil business," said Garth, smiling in her direction.

"The nuns will value her expertise," said XT wryly.

"Right," she replied, rolling her eyes.

"There'll be other old holding tanks and oil wells buried nearby," said Garth. "According to Aunt Jane, there used to be fifteen or so active wells on this property, and you can see by the number of remaining pump jacks that there are only six in operation today."

"Yeah," said XT. "Apparently they buried wells when they ceased to be productive. I've heard they're all over the county."

"There's an approved process for dealing with abandoned wells," said Garth. "They're supposed to remove the tubing and fill sections of well bore with concrete to separate gas and water zones from each other. Then the wellhead and casing are cut off and a cap is welded in place before they bury the whole thing."

He looked at Hilma. "Did I get that right?" he asked.

"Pretty close," she replied with a straight face.

"I bet several wells were abandoned without going through proper process," said XT.

"You can just imagine," agreed Graeme.

"Do you suppose the existing wells need much maintenance?" asked XT.

"I'm sure Aunt Jane can fill us in on details," said Garth.

"We should pay a visit to Charlie. He has more than three hundred active oil wells on his Oil Springs property," suggested XT.

"Those wells are still connected by jerker lines like his great-grandfather's were," added Graeme. It was well known among local residents that in the 1860s, oil pioneer John Fairbank was the first to use an ingenious system of pulleys and shafts allowing many wells to be pumped from a single power source.

"The abbey's wells also use jerker lines," said Garth.

"Come over here and see one of them," called XT who had been wandering through the tall flora. They gathered near him, noticing that the growth in this area was cleared to enable the wood and iron mechanism to slide slowly back and forth, back and forth.

"Are you ready to check out the abbey?" asked the police constable of his fellow investors.

Scarcely able to conceal their eagerness, they picked their way through weeds and wildflowers towards the elegant old manor. Hilma followed, finding their excitement contagious.

"From what you've both told me, the main building will require extensive repairs," said Graeme.

"New plumbing and electrical wiring for starters," said XT.

"And new roofing," added Garth. "Individual slates have been replaced through the years as leaks developed, but Aunt Jane says it's past time for the entire roof to be re-slated. When we make the rounds, you'll notice water stains in the plaster, especially on the topmost floor."

"Would we be using slate again?" wondered XT. "We'd want to keep at least the façade of the abbey as authentic as possible."

"I've been doing a bit of research," said Garth. "As you'd expect, slate is expensive and heavy. However, there are some lighter rubber and metal products available now."

"And they look like slate?" asked Graeme.

"Realistically so," said Garth. "And apparently you can walk on a roof with rubber or metal slates whereas real slate tends to crack."

Garth rang the bell at the garden gate to summon the porter. In no time Sister Helen appeared and led them along the cloister walkway into the kitchen. "I'm to take you through to Mother Abbess, but feel free to ask questions along the way," she said.

"All the appliances in working order?" asked Graeme glancing around the well-polished galley.

"Oh, yes. We prioritize everything in the few rooms we use," she replied.

"Great woodwork," noted XT, running his hand along the wainscoting as they followed the porter along the narrow corridors.

"Solid plaster," said Graeme, tapping on a wall.

When they reached the parlour, Sister Helen explained that, with most of the abbey unused, the sisters spent most of their free time in that cozy little room.

"I thought there was a television in here," said XT, recalling his previous visit.

Wordlessly, the nun slid back a wall panel above the fireplace to reveal an entertainment centre complete with a television and various electronic devices.

"We like keeping up with the news and listening to music, but we don't like the visibility of modern contraptions distracting us from quiet reflection," she explained.

In the chapel, she allowed for time to absorb the ambience of the beautiful place before ushering them to the abbess's study.

"Aunt Jane, I'd like you to meet a potential investment partner, Graeme Kilgour," said Garth when they entered the room. "Graeme will be teaching art at the high school in Providence Crossing starting in September and moving from Wickford over the summer."

"Very pleased to meet you," said the abbess, rising to shake his hand. "A partnership comprised of nuns, an art teacher, a physician and a police constable should make a creative team."

"It certainly should," agreed Graeme.

"So, gentlemen, what are your impressions so far?" asked the abbess.

"It's going to be a big project," said XT, "but the abbey is so charming that it will be a labour of love."

"It does my heart good to hear you say that," said the abbess. "I was afraid you'd be deterred by the deterioration of the place."

"It's a wonderful heritage building begging to be revived," said XT.

"We were wondering who does maintenance on the wells now that Claude's gone," said Garth.

"Claude was only responsible for clearing weeds and snow away from the jerker lines," said the abbess. "There's a man down the road who checks on the wells periodically and does repair work on the jerker lines. But mostly the pumps work away with minimal supervision."

"How much oil do your six wells produce?"

"Approximately six barrels every five days. It's carried by underground pipes to the road where it's pumped into an oil truck every couple of weeks."

"So the wells are worth maintaining," said her great-nephew.

"Oh, yes. They provided a welcome supplement for this old abbey."

"What part of the abbey are you planning to live in once renovations begin, Abbess?" asked Graeme.

The west end of the first and second floors, hopefully. We want access to the chapel and gardens."

"We'll need to run an elevator from the main to the third floors," said XT. "Do you have any thoughts where it might go?"

"Come with me," said the abbess, leading them to the foyer with its marvelous curving stairway, impressive front doors and lovely stain glass transom.

"Whoa!" said Graeme, awed at seeing it for the first time. "This is beautiful! But surely an elevator would ruin it."

"It could," said the abbess. "Which is why we will need the assistance of an architect to help us plan a functionally appealing front hall."

"Do you mind if we show Graeme upstairs?" asked XT.

"Go right ahead," said the abbess. "I'll go back to my study."

"What a wonderful place you have," said Graeme. "No wonder my wife was impressed."

"Speaking of your wife," said the abbess, "you'll find Dillian upstairs with Azur in the first room on the left."

"What!" exclaimed Graeme.

"Our wives are upstairs?" asked XT. "How did they get here?"

"Bram dropped them off while you were in the meadow," said the abbess. "I let them in through the front doors."

"That's why we didn't see a car," said Garth. "Did you know about this?" he asked Hilma.

Hilma smiled in satisfaction. All morning she'd been bursting with her knowledge of the surprise plotted out by her sister and her devious friend.

Bemused, the men climbed the elegant old staircase to the second floor and entered the door to the left of the landing.

"Okay, ladies, where are you?" called XT.

"In here," sang out Azur's voice.

They followed the voice to the closest cell on the window side of the corridor and stopped in amazement at the sight that greeted them. Hilma lingered in the hallway to hear what would transpire.

The little room had been transformed into a welcoming café. The window had been thrown open admitting fresh summer breezes and the twittering of birds. Beneath the window, a vase of blue cornflowers and delphinium had been placed alongside a floating candle on a small desk. Pushed against the wall, a cot was casually draped in colourful throws and cushions.

In the centre of the room, a linen-covered table was set for six. The menu consisted of lobster pasta, herb croissants and red wine served in long stemmed goblets.

"What is this?" asked XT.

"Welcome, gentlemen," said Dilly brightly. "Sit down while the croissants are still warm. You too, Hilma."

"We haven't finished the tour," protested Graeme.

"That can wait till after lunch," said Azur.

"How did you manage this?" asked XT without a lot of enthusiasm.

"We had help from Sister Colleen and Sister Martha," explained his wife. "Aren't you pleased?" she asked, looking wounded.

"Well, yes. It's just that today was for preliminary poking around and thinking things over."

"And you can't do your *preliminary poking and thinking* with us here?" asked Dilly, her voice having lost its former brightness.

"And you don't need to eat while conducting your preliminary whatever?" asked Azur.

"Perhaps Hilma and I should leave the four of you alone," said Garth.

"Stay right here, Garth," said Dilly. "You and Hilma are included in this luncheon date."

Obligingly, they seated themselves around the little table, the men uncertainly, the women disappointed at the lukewarm response to their careful plans.

"Okay, guys," admitted Azur finally. "We did have an ulterior motive in wanting to serve you lunch before you completed your abbey tour."

"And the ulterior motive would be…?" wondered Graeme, clearly mystified.

How dense can men be? Hilma wondered in amusement.

"I'm waiting," said XT.

The women exchanged sheepish looks.

"I think I get it," said Garth suddenly. "The ladies have fallen in love with the abbey and want to live here."

"Is that right?" demanded XT.

Azur bit her lip and nodded. The men exchanged incredulous glances.

Hilma sat in suspenseful silence.

"You know what? I like the idea," said Graeme unexpectedly. "Dil and I have to find a place near Providence Crossing anyway. Why not make it a condo at Black Springs?"

Dillian stifled a gasp of disbelief.

Azur looked inquiringly at her husband.

"I can't believe I'm saying this, but yes, the idea has merit," said XT cautiously.

Eight

Encouraged by the plans of family and friends to have abbey condos, Hilma decided to go ahead with a trial move and begin orientation with the nuns.

The title assigned to her by the abbess was *Business Manager*, a role which the sisters said would evolve over time. Orientation would be more like an apprenticeship, she was told. Initially, she would spend time individually with each sister, including the abbess herself, to become familiar with the workings of the abbey.

The abbess had suggested that she bring her belongings during the morning and be ready to join the community by lunchtime. After lunch, she would be assigned to the porter and herbist, Sister Helen.

Hilma's grandmother assured her that anticipation was more stressful than plunging right into a new environment. "You're handling this well," she told her granddaughter as she helped her pack bedding, clothing and personal items for the move.

"I'm doing fine, Mavis," Hilma replied. Actually, the thought of embracing a productive future after five years of dependency was invigorating.

"Will you be bringing your iPad?"

"Yes, and my cell phone."

"What about snacks and beverages?" asked Bram, standing at the ready to load bags and boxes into the car.

"There's a kitchenette just down the hall from my room with a fridge, toaster, kettle and microwave," said Hilma. "Sister

Colleen told me I can bring anything I want up from the main kitchen and keep it in the fridge."

They arrived at the abbey mid-morning and were admitted by Sister Helen who fussed over Mavis, their old midwife, before leading them up to the second floor.

"The room next to yours is for your cello and harp," the porter reminded Hilma.

"We brought her cello today," said Bram. "But we're getting movers for the harp."

As soon as the porter left, Mavis and Hilma made up the cot, topping it with a rose comforter edged with blue flowers and a matching throw pillow.

"The room looks homier already," said Bram encouragingly.

The women hung sweaters, blouses and t-shirts in the closet along with a summer jacket and a long skirt. In the chest of drawers, they placed folded jeans, underwear, socks and personal items.

Hilma's window overlooked an expanse of vines, shrubbery and wildflowers, and gazing through it, Mavis felt a wonderful peace. *This will be a place of healing for my granddaughter*, she thought. Aloud she said, "I guess we'll be going now dear. We'll see you on the weekend when Bram comes to pick you up."

Hilma smiled and hugged her grandparents good-bye. *I will be fine*, she told herself, trying to ignore the butterflies in her stomach.

Bram and Mavis had barely exited the abbey when chimes rang melodiously through the abbey. Believing it to be a summons to lunch, Hilma went down the back stairs into the kitchen. There was no one there although the aroma of baked rolls and chicken vegetable soup suffused the room. Finding the refectory also vacant, she walked out into the hall and followed a murmur of voices to the chapel. The sisters were at prayer.

Embarrassed at intruding, she backed into the hall and stood there uncertainly. Minutes later, Sister Colleen emerged from the chapel on her way to the kitchen. She smiled at Hilma and told her that lunch would be served momentarily.

Soon the other sisters filed into the refectory, recited a blessing and served themselves from the side table. This time the novices were present but Sister Martha was at her office.

"Eula doesn't eat with you?" asked Hilma, disappointed that the writer wasn't there for moral support.

"She prefers to eat breakfast and lunch alone although she usually joins us for supper," said Sister Jamini.

Over lunch, the sisters filled Hilma in on abbey routine. "We follow canonical hours throughout the day," explained the abbess. "Since the Middle Ages, monastic life followed the ancient Jewish practice of praying seven times a day. The canonical hours are traditionally called Matins, Lauds, Terce, Sext, None, Vespers and Compline."

"In modern times, the hours have been modified," said Sister Beatrice. "We no longer get up at midnight for Matins, the Office of Readings. Instead, we do these readings in our own rooms when the chimes wake us at five-thirty. Then we get dressed and come down for Lauds, also called Morning Prayer, before we go to breakfast around seven-twenty."

"By the way, Hilma, you aren't expected to attend prayer with us," said the abbess. "You can feel free to pray however and whenever you choose."

"If I'm in the middle of planting and my hands are all dirty, I occasionally stay outside and do my own mid-morning praying," Sister Helen confided. "However, I do come in for midday prayer before lunch."

"In the days when the abbey was filled with sisters, silence was observed at meals and someone would be assigned to read spiritual works while food was being served and eaten," said Sister Beatrice. "That was on top of the canonical hours."

Words floated around Hilma making little sense. "Should I be writing this down?" she asked anxiously.

"No," laughed Sister Colleen. "Just learn which chimes signal the imminence of mealtimes and all will be well."

"Before today's over, you'll hear chimes for None at three in the afternoon and again at five-thirty for Vespers," said Sister Beatrice, not willing to give up on a proper introduction to liturgy. "For Compline at nine, we have the choice of coming to the chapel or praying Night Prayer privately in our cell before retiring for the night."

"Any more, it's just Beatrice and the novices who go to chapel that late. The rest of us are exempt by reason of age," said Sister Colleen with a smile.

"As if I'm not as old as the rest of you!" sniffed Sister Beatrice. "And what's Martha's excuse?"

Under the abbess' steady gaze, the organist lowered her eyes to her plate.

"So what time should I get up in the morning?" asked Hilma, trying to get to the gist of things pertaining to her own routine.

"You can ignore the five-thirty chimes but when you hear them again at ten to seven, you'll know that Morning Prayer will begin in ten minutes and breakfast will follow twenty minutes later," said the abbess. "The bells are very reliable."

"Or I can set my alarm clock," said Hilma.

"You could," said Sister Helen, "but I predict you'll soon find it easier to rely on the bells."

"Who rings the bells?"

"The chimes are automatic unless there's a power failure. Then the porter rings a hand bell like in the old days," said the abbess.

With lunch finished, Hilma followed Sister Helen into the cloister garden.

"In the days when we had lots of helping hands, this entire area was ablaze with wonderful flowers from early spring to late autumn. But in recent years, I've simplified it," she said.

"It looks beautiful to me," Hilma said.

"We have thirty varieties of hosta and almost as many daylilies," said the herbist. "They don't need a lot of care other than weeding."

The young woman nodded and trailed the nun along an elongated vegetable garden laid out with ordered rows of herbs, peas, beans, carrots, beets and potatoes. Along one wall were raspberry bushes, apple, cherry and pear trees and a strawberry patch in its final stages of picking. Roses, hollyhocks and vines climbed the back wall in random tangles.

"In the spring, our greenhouse is bursting with seedlings and wee plants," said Sister Helen, leading her towards the back wall. "And in this corner we have rhubarb and asparagus. Tomorrow we can bring in some of both for Colleen. Fortunately, she loves baking, cooking and preserving as much as I love gardening."

"Where would you like me to start?" asked Hilma.

"You can pick the last of the strawberries today, and do some weeding in the vegetable garden," said the nun. "First though, we'll do a bit of exploring. We enter our little cemetery through the archway beside the greenhouse. Then we'll go out to the meadow."

Since repetition was reassuring as well as instructive, Hilma didn't mention that she'd been shown these places on yesterday's tour with the abbess. They entered the cemetery and wandered amongst the white crosses marking the simple graves.

It was then Hilma noticed a girl with short fair hair near the rose bushes surrounding the Holy Family statue. She glanced questioningly at Sister Helen, but the girl disappeared without eliciting any reaction from the nun. Disturbed, Hilma followed the gardener back to the garden and through the gate to the fields and buildings beyond the walls. Midst grasses and wildflowers, pump jacks bobbed slowly up and down.

"As you can see, our meadow extends all the way to the evergreens in the distance," said Sister Helen as they wandered leisurely through a field awash in the scents of flowers and grasses. Bees buzzed and butterflies fluttered among yellow coreopsis, black-eyed Susan, feather reed grass, mauve bee balm, copper crowned echinacea and clumps of oxeye daisies. There were tall spikes of blazing star on slender stalks, white sprays of wild quinine, blue and violet coneflowers and sweet-smelling alfalfa.

"This looks like milkweed," noted Hilma, examining some rose and purple flowers clustered at the tops of their leafy stems.

"Common milkweed," agreed the nun. "We have to look after our monarch butterflies."

"It's all wonderful," sighed Hilma, having mostly recovered from seeing the girl in the cemetery.

"You missed last month's daffodils and wild poppies," smiled the nun, apparently pleased that Hilma shared her passion for nature. "It was a breathtaking vision."

"Are you personally involved in keeping this meadow so beautiful?"

"Every year or so, I sprinkle seeds around randomly, especially poppy seeds. They seem to start thinning out if I don't. Martha helped me the last couple of times. She likes to get out in the fresh air whenever she can get away from her office and court appearances. Mostly though, the meadow is looked after by the Creator."

"Will you be with me in the cloister garden?"

"I seem to be always out there puttering around," replied the nun.

"But will I ever be alone?"

Sister Helen appraised the young woman thoughtfully. "Do you want more time by yourself?" she asked.

"No," replied Hilma in a small quavery voice, ashamed of her vulnerability.

"There will always be someone near then," said the nun reassuringly.

Nine

By early July, renovation plans were progressing. Seated around the long cherry wood table in the abbey library, architect, John Bolen, updated the management team. Present on this occasion were all seven nuns along with Garth, XT and Graeme.

Hilma was there too in her budding role of Business Manager, a role she was gradually accepting, having been reassured that her basic responsibility was shielding the sisters from external interactions. Sister Martha was an anomaly being out and about, and even she seemed to savour abbey seclusion whenever possible.

"I understand that Bernie will be arriving shortly," said the architect. Bernard Hansen was the co-owner of a local construction company operated by the Hansen brothers.

"He had an on-site situation to attend to on the way," explained the abbess.

"Any questions or comments while we're waiting?" asked John.

"All the third-floor condos have been pre-sold thanks to your firm's artistic renditions of the abbey," said Garth.

"And your creative marketing," added the architect.

"Sister Martha's legal expertise played no small role," added XT, nodding to the nun who smiled back in acknowledgement.

"Who are your buyers?" asked John.

"As you know, three of the large corner units have been claimed by XT and Azur, Graeme and Dilly and yours truly," said Garth.

"The fourth corner has been purchased by a retired couple from Toronto, and the three smaller units by a Canadian writer living part-time in France, a couple from Arizona looking for a unique summer place, and two actors with apartments in New York and Paris," added XT.

"They seem to all be people seeking a haven from their complex lives," noted the abbess. "I get the impression that they'll spend only short periods of time here each year."

"Oh, here's Bernie now!" said John Bolen as the contractor entered the room and took a place at the table. "Now all of you realize," continued the architect, "that this is going to be an on-going construction project. After today, you'll be seeing less of me and a whole lot more of Bernie and his crew."

"We'll be ready to start next week," said Bernie, "so I appreciate being invited for an update."

"I'm going to start with a review of the present abbey," said the architect, clicking on his laptop to display a third-storey floor plan on a wall screen. He pointed out that, as on the second floor, a U- shaped corridor fronted the cells along both sides and across the back. He showed his audience where stairs descended from the back corner to the kitchen on the ground floor.

"There's currently a row of bathing rooms, toilets and service rooms running down the centre," he pointed out. "This will be replaced with a corridor going from the elevator to the various condos."

"Will the back stairs remain?" asked Garth.

"Yes, for safety and fire regulation reasons, and also because they add to the building's heritage charm. Incidentally, all hallways throughout the remodeled abbey will imitate the plaster and ornamental wood trim that they currently have."

"How many separate condo designs are there?" asked the contractor.

"Four basic ones with unlimited options for each," said John. "Construction will start with the three corner ones owned by the partners while the others will be roughed in for the time being."

"Am I correct that my crews will be working simultaneously on the first and third floors?"

"That's right," agreed John.

"And of course we'll need to install the elevator in order to access the third floor."

"When will the initial renovations be completed?" asked Sister Martha.

"In three or four months if all goes smoothly," said Bernie.

"And the remaining condos?"

"The purchasers have been told their condos will be completed in two years."

Sister Martha asked about the retreat area planned for the second floor, and was told that it should be completed late the next summer.

"We'll begin there as soon as the current occupants move to their condos," said the contractor. "In the meantime, the second-floor kitchenette will be rewired to handle additional appliances. We've also been instructed to wire for washers and dryers in one of the empty cells and an entertainment centre in another."

"I've been told my kitchen will disappear during the renovations," said Sister Colleen.

"As will the big old laundry," said the architect. "Your new downstairs quarters will be modern and efficient."

"In the meantime, your work space on the second floor will be more compact," the abbess reminded her. "Perhaps you'll find some time for relaxation."

Sister Colleen raised a dubious eyebrow.

"In time, there will be a business office on the main floor," said the architect. "Also a few of the lovely old rooms at the front of the abbey will be accessible to retreatants and condo owners as part of the abbey experience."

"Everyone will appreciate that," said Graeme.

"For the safety of those living on the second floor, we'll be blocking off the east end while we work on the foyer and elevator," said the contractor. "And since you'll be using the back stairs to exit the building, we have to make a doorway in the kitchen wall near the back stairwell."

"Does that mean we'll have to enter our garden from the outside?" asked Sister Helen.

"Only until your remodeled quarters are ready for you," said Bernie.

"Will the side doorway be permanent?" asked XT.

"Yes, it will remain as the back fire exit for the two upper floors. As for the sisters, once their area is finished, they will again be able to use the original door into the cloister garden."

"Any other thoughts, Bernie, before I leave?" asked John.

"I notice that you're calling for an expanded parking area with car ports along one side."

"Yes," said the architect. "We felt that ivy-covered car ports would add to the ambience more so than a garage."

"Any comments or questions, Hilma?" asked the abbess, drawing her new manager into the conversation.

Hilma shuffled the papers on the table before her, willing herself to behave in a professional manner. She found it distracting to know that Garth was watching her performance.

"I see from your plans that each unit will have a separate electrical box and water meter," she noted. "Will utilities in the rest of the abbey be handled similarly?"

"Good question, Hilma," said the architect. "The electricians will sort out the details, of course, but it's my understanding that the first and second floors will have single utility systems."

"That's correct," said Garth, causing her to shift her concentration in his direction.

"So communal areas of the abbey plus exterior lighting, fountains et cetera will be covered by single costing schedules?"

"Yes, and it's our intent that condo sales and fees will largely cover this," added Garth.

He smiled at Hilma, and although she allowed her eyes to smile back, she had to bite her lower lip to contain unrestrained laughter. *Why does his presence turn me into a giddy school girl when it would be so wrong to lead him on?* she thought.

"Did you notice when you arrived today that the landscapers have been hard at work?" asked the abbess of all present.

"XT and I went over to talk with them," said Graeme. He related that the landscapers told them they were laying flagstone paths into the front wooded section. Next they'll wind walkways around the sheds at the back and extend them into the back meadow. Trees and shrubs will be planted throughout the property.

"There'll be arbours, gazebos and a large fountain when they're finished," added XT.

"And the weeds and brush covering the labyrinth at the far end of the meadow will be cleared away," said the abbess.

"I'm looking forward to walking the labyrinth," said Sister Martha. "I have yet to even see it."

"It's been years since anyone's seen it," said Sister Beatrice.

The meeting concluded and one by one each person left until only Garth and the abbess remained in the library.

"Aunt Jane, I've got my house up for sale to free up some money," Garth told his great-aunt. "Would it be okay if I put my furniture in storage and took a spare cell on the second floor?"

"Of course it's perfectly fine," said the abbess. "I'll put you on the north side with the Kilgours. That's on the opposite corridor from Hilma."

"I wish I could get as close to Hilma as you seem to think I can," said her nephew, sighing.

"Everything in God's time," she said.

"By the way, I have a dog," he said hesitantly.

"Helen will be thrilled. The novices too. When our old border collie, Suzy, died during the winter, we couldn't believe how sad we all felt. We've already asked the humane society to keep us in mind for a suitable replacement. What breed is your dog?"

"Doberman."

"A good watchdog I bet."

"People who don't know Shadow tend to be wary because of his size and loud bark. But he's a rescue dog and kind of a suck."

"You'll have to introduce him gradually to our cats and chickens," cautioned the abbess. "We can't have any harm coming to them."

"Will he be allowed inside the abbey?"

"As long as he's well behaved," said his great-aunt. "Suzy roamed the abbey as if she were one of us."

"Shadow is very obedient," said Garth. "However, as long as I'm living on the second floor, I'll either take him to work with me or put him in one of your sheds whenever I'm away."

"Does Hilma like Shadow?" asked the abbess.

"She shows the dog more affection than she does me."

"Then she'll probably be happy to keep an eye on him while you're on duty."

"Perhaps," said Garth.

"Life in the abbey will never be the same," said the abbess.

"Are you sorry you committed to this venture?" asked Garth.

"Not for a moment," she said.

Ten

Apart from a mid-morning break for freshly-squeezed lemonade in the kitchen followed by Terce in the chapel, Sister Helen and Hilma spent the mornings weeding and collecting herbs in the cloister garden.

Hilma found it restful to attend mid-morning prayer, listening to the drone of nuns reciting psalms. Since no one expected her to participate, she was free to absorb the peace and lose herself in unbridled flights of thought before returning to work.

But on this day, Terce was long past and the relentless sun flamed high in a cloudless sky. Wilting in the July heat, Hilma marvelled at the older woman's stamina.

"I believe we've done a good day's work, don't you?" asked the nun as if reading the young woman's thoughts. "I think you deserve the remainder of the day off. Naturally, I can't speak for Beatrice. She may insist on a lesson, but you can always shorten your after-lesson practice time in the chapel."

"What will *you* be doing?" asked Hilma.

"I'm going to take some of these herbs in to Colleen and spread the rest on drying screens. Run along now."

"Will you be taking the afternoon off?" asked Hilma, setting down her spade and rising gratefully to her feet.

"One of the blessings of old age is being able to pace yourself without feeling guilty," said the nun. "I may just spend the afternoon reading in the parlour."

Rather than go inside, Hilma exited through the garden gate and walked around the side of the abbey to watch two workers pounding an opening into the kitchen wall. At regular intervals they drilled new holes into the mortar before picking up their sledge hammers for another round of pounding.

"Seems to be solid," noted Hilma.

"These old buildings were made to last," agreed one of the men, stopping to take a sip from his water bottle.

"We'll have the doorway framed before we leave today, and by tomorrow night you'll have a proper exit for your back stairs," said the other man.

"Will it have a door by then?" asked Hilma, wondering how long the abbey would have unsecured access.

"Sure will," he replied, picking up the drill and returning to his task.

To fill in the remaining time gap before lunch, Hilma set off for the back of property. She peeked into a shed containing neatly stacked rakes, shovels and other landscaping tools. A larger shed housed the tractor and a smaller riding lawn mower.

As she was preparing to visit the chicken coop, she was drawn to movement in the meadow. Turning in that direction, Hilma saw a girl running through the fields. When Hilma called out to her, she stopped and turned around, revealing that she held a baby close to her chest. The girl looked at Hilma with dark, searching eyes before fading away.

Hilma shivered though the sun burned hot overhead. She hurried back to the abbey, relieved that men working on the thick brick wall provided normalcy to the day.

Before she was able to unlatch the gate, a familiar blue Volvo pulled into the driveway, spewing stones from its braking wheels.

XT had barely stepped from the car when Hilma threw herself at him, hugging him tightly.

"Whoa!" he said. "I haven't even shared the news with you."

"What news?" she asked, drawing back.

"You have two beautiful nieces whom your sister can't wait for you to meet."

Hilma burst into tears.

"Are you alright?" asked XT.

Hilma nodded mutely, unwilling to talk about her recent experience in the meadow. Her family and friends were so hopeful that she was regaining some of her former vivacity that she hesitated to unsettle them with accounts of spectral sightings. She had already experienced Garth's inability to see the woman in the flats and none of the nuns seemed to see the girls around the abbey.

When Hilma found her voice, she asked XT if he would please tell Sister Helen to relay a message to Sister Beatrice that she would be away for the afternoon.

"Are you not happy at the abbey?" asked XT as they drove off towards Creekside.

"Everyone's pleasant enough and I'm enjoying my work there," she replied, trying to discreetly wipe tears from her eyes.

"How are the organ lessons going?"

"The ogre isn't saying much, but I get the feeling she's reluctantly impressed. I don't think she knows about the extraordinary speed at which Sensos absorb things."

"Then what is it?"

"I can't wait to see Azur and the babies," she answered evasively.

"They're beautiful," said the proud father.

"Aren't they early?" asked Hilma.

"Only two weeks which is not unusual for twins. And they're both perfect."

"Were they born at Warren Avenue as you planned?"

"Yes, delivered by midwife Mavis. I was on standby, a nervous wreck."

"And were you able to remain on standby?"

"I managed until the very end when one of the babies seemed reluctant to cry. So I might have done a bit of suctioning," he admitted sheepishly.

"I doubt that Mavis minded."

"Actually, I think she appreciated assistance since there were two of the little critters along with their mother to attend to."

"Was it a long labour?"

"Long enough. I'll definitely be sticking to neurology."

"When will I learn the babies' names?" asked Hilma as they reached the residential area known as Crescent Park. Azur had insisted that they not name the babes until she held them in her arms.

"We'll tell you while you're meeting them," said her brother-in-law, pulling into the driveway at the large white residence on Warren Avenue where her grandparents lived.

This was the place where, surrounded by the love and discipline of Bram and Mavis, Hilma and her sister had grown up. A place they still called home. The lovely square house had tall multi-paned windows, a low angled roof and boxed cornices with brackets. Ornate gingerbread adorned the verandah which wrapped around the home's front and side.

Hilma jumped out of the car, rushed through the front door and raced up the winding oak stairway. She followed the sound of voices into the room that had been Azur's when she lived at home. Propped upright with pillows, her sister's smiling face was bent over two blanketed babies. The doting great-grandparents of the new arrivals hovered nearby.

Hilma gave Bram and Mavis affectionate pecks on their weathered cheeks before approaching her sister and brand-new nieces.

Azur raised her face for a kiss. "Would you like to hold them?" she asked.

Hilma gently took the bundled offerings from her sister and, assisted by XT, settled into a padded rocker. Responding to the change in position, the infants whimpered softly and waved their tiny arms. One wee fist latched onto her aunt's proffered finger. Although their eyelids fluttered and their lips trembled, the infants remained asleep.

"You're just in time for the official naming," said Azur.

"I can't wait," said Hilma. "You've kept me is suspense so long!"

"Our firstborn is Mavis Violet," said her sister.

"Good choice," said Hilma, smiling at her grandmother who beamed back.

"Also named after Bram's great-aunt, Violet Galvinston, whom we met during our adventure in Prosper Station," added her sister.

"And the other one?"

"Sarah Jane," said XT happily. "Sarah for my mother and great-grandmother, Sarah Tennyson. Jane for Mavis' grandmother, Jane McConnell."

"Both of whom you met on your adventure in Prosper Station while I was imprisoned in Vapourlea," said Hilma, her eyes filling with tears.

"But you were rescued from there, dear, and that's all behind us," said Mavis quickly, not wanting her younger granddaughter to spoil this happy occasion.

It will never be behind me, thought Hilma. Aloud she said, "They're beautiful names for gorgeous babies. How can you tell them apart?"

"Mavis Violet has a heart-shaped birthmark on her right wrist," said Azur.

Hilma searched until she found the tiny heart on one baby wrist. "Mavis and Sarah," she said, admiringly.

"How will you distinguish between your Mavises — apart from our ages?" asked Mavis.

"You're going to have to settle for Gramma Mavis," said Azur.

"You know, Sweetie, I'm honoured to have the little one named for me, but I think you should call her by her second name."

"Violet?"

"Look at her," said Mavis, walking over to touch her namesake's soft little hand. "Precious like a lovely little flower, a wee violet."

XT said he loved all the names chosen for his daughters. However, on hearing Mavis' suggestion, he conceded that Violet would be nice.

"What about calling her Vi?" he asked his wife.

"Vi," said Azur, testing the name. "I like it. A pixy version of Violet."

"It suits her," agreed Mavis.

"They have such shiny black hair," said XT, standing over his new daughters.

"It looks bluish to me," said Hilma.

"Hmm," said Mavis, scrutinizing the infants' hair. "Let me take them to their mother for her opinion." She gently extracted them from Hilma and carried them to the bed.

"What do you think?" she asked her older granddaughter.

"I believe it's indigo," said Azur, running her fingers over the little heads.

"Indeed," agreed Mavis. "The colour of their mother's primary aura reflecting wisdom, insight, intuition and mystical enlightenment. These are special children."

"Mrroow," said the family cat, Bleu, jumping onto the bed.

"Come take a peek, Bleu," invited Azur. "Do you like our babies?"

The cat chirped and purred approvingly before jumping to the floor.

"I wonder what colour their auras will be?" wondered the new mother.

"Auras develop with maturity," said Mavis. "We'll have to be patient."

"Don't you feel we're missing something, Bram?" XT asked his grandfather-in-law. "We're both carriers of the sensointuitive gene but we lack special abilities including being able to visualize auras."

"It's just as well," said Bram. "Some of us have to stay grounded in the mundane."

"I don't see auras either," Hilma reminded them.

"It's okay, sweetheart," said her grandmother. "You were the first to notice the babies' hair colour. See, your intuitions and other senses are compensating."

"Are you able to see the indigo hair?" Azur asked her husband hopefully.

"Now that it's been pointed out, yes," said XT.

"I see it too," said Bram, smiling in awe.

Eleven

Although Ethel Witherton invited them to stay with her until their condo was ready, Dillian knew that her mother was secretly relieved when they insisted that accommodations at the abbey would be fine.

By the Kilgours' moving day, the abbey's elevator had not yet been installed, and would not, in any case, be available for several weeks. Thus, even with the bulk of their belongings crammed into Mrs. Witherton's garage, it took many trips up the abbey back stairs to have essential clothing and supplies brought to their temporary dwelling on the second floor.

Hilma was on hand to watch the children because the abbess had decreed that attending to new tenants was within the realm of her managerial position.

Dillian and Graeme told their children they would be camping in the abbey for the summer, and Meredith and Gideon were beside themselves with delight.

"Did you know we would be camping with you, Hilma?" asked Meri.

"That's so exciting!" replied Hilma.

"And did you know that you were babysitting us today?"

"I did!" she said with feigned enthusiasm.

"But really, you only need to babysit Gideon," said Meri. "I have to help Mommy and Daddy unpack."

"Do you think you could stay with Gideon and me for a while until your little brother gets used to his new surroundings?"

asked Hilma, having promised the child's parents to keep an eye on the children for the morning.

Needing Meri's help with Gideon was partly true anyway since the toddler was already fussing as his father tried to harness him into a stroller.

"Oh yes, Meri," said Graeme. "We're counting on you to help Hilma with your little brother."

"Okay," agreed the child after a moment's hesitation.

Dilly and Graeme had acquired possession of three adjacent cells as well as a nearby bathing room, toilet and dining cell. One of the cells would become their bedroom, another, the children's and the third, a sitting room. The family would share the kitchenette, laundry and entertainment room with other second floor occupants.

With Gideon in his stroller and Meri at her side, Hilma set off along the corridor on an improvised tour. When she showed the children where their tub and toilet were, Meri expressed surprise that these bathroom fixtures were in separate rooms.

"This way, someone can be having a bath while others use the toilet," Hilma explained.

"Will our condo be like this?" asked Meri.

"I'm sure it will be quite different," said Hilma.

They visited the entertainment room and the kitchenette where Sister Colleen was busy preparing food. Then Hilma took the children to the five cells which had been converted to small dining rooms.

"This is where the sisters eat," she said, indicating the cell nearest the infirmary at the far west end. "And the one beside it is where I eat with Eula and Sister Jamini and Sister Fazeela."

"Where will I eat?"

"Right next door," said Hilma, taking them into the adjoining cell.

"Our dining room has a sink!" said Meri.

"Some of the original rooms do have sinks," said Hilma. *Perfect for mealtime with young children*, she thought.

"Look! There's your highchair, Gideon. And there's my booster seat," exclaimed Meri.

"Highchair," said Gideon, struggling to climb out of his stroller.

"Not yet, Gideon," Hilma told the toddler. "First I'm going to show you my room and then we'll get cookies from the kitchenette."

Meri ran alongside as Hilma pushed the stroller up to a newly-installed gate across the west hall between the exit stairs and the sisters' quarters.

"Why is there a gate here?" asked Meri.

"The sisters' area is private," explained Hilma. "Everything your family needs is on your corridor. But I'm going to take you through the private area to show you my room."

She opened the gate and led the children past the sisters' rooms and onto the south corridor.

"This is Sister Jamini's room and this is Sister Fazeela's room and this is Eula's room," she said as they went by each unit.

"Can we go in and see them?"

"No, the sisters are working and Eula is writing," said Hilma quietly, not wishing to disturb the writer. "But you can see my room which is just like theirs."

Inside Hilma's unit, Meri walked about examining everything. Hilma sat down in her armchair while the child explored.

"It's like a hotel room," said Meri.

"Cookie, cookie," said Gideon, twisting about in his stroller.

"He wants a cookie," translated Meri. "I do too."

Because of the children's eagerness for a snack, Hilma decided to curtail the tour and not show them the temporary offices further down the hall. They returned the way they came and discovered in the kitchenette that Sister Colleen had already set cookies and milk on a tray for the children as well as a mug of coffee for Hilma.

"I'll carry it for you because you've got your hands full," said the nun, bustling ahead to the Kilgours' dining cell.

Gideon was happy to trade stroller for highchair, and Meri seemed to consider it an adventure to sit in her familiar booster seat atop an abbey chair.

After their snack, they went to the entertainment room. Hilma found a children's program on television that met with Meri's approval and which Gideon seemed content to watch. Soon, however, Meri announced that it was time for her to help her parents unpack and ran off to find them.

Reluctantly Hilma followed, holding the toddler's hand to prevent him from taking off in the opposite direction. They found Graeme standing in the doorway of one of their cells, his arms full of clothing. He was breathing heavily from the exertion of climbing the back stairs.

"I thought we were bringing a minimum of things," he grumbled, winking at Hilma.

"This *is* a minimum," insisted his wife, sitting on an unmade bed to catch her breath. "It's no different than going to a cottage for three months. Not that we've ever done that."

"Yes, and people always take more than they need on any holiday," said Graeme.

"You'll thank me when you're looking for something you want," said Dilly.

"Unless it's amongst the stuff we left in your mother's garage."

"Weren't you just complaining that we'd brought too much?"

"Just kidding," muttered Graeme.

When Meri informed her parents that she was now ready to help them, they suggested she unpack her own clothing and toys. Hilma took the children into the adjoining cell where a dresser and crib had been set up. Several boxes and a toy bin had been deposited on the floor near the single bed.

Hilma opened boxes for the children and they began to pull things out, happily exclaiming over each item as if it were a newly discovered treasure. Her patience was severely tested when she tried to guide their efforts in putting everything in proper places. In the end, while Meri played with a doll and Gideon rolled a truck over the wooden floorboards, it was Hilma who put things where she thought they might go. Thus it was with great relief that Hilma heard the cook's hand bell summoning them to lunch.

Having taken possession of the kitchenette after being ousted from her large downstairs kitchen, Sister Colleen contentedly bustled about in her temporary domain with its new aluminum refrigerator, range and oven, and even more amazingly, a matching dishwasher and compact freezer.

Although the Kilgours had originally been invited to use the kitchenette whenever they wished, a compromise had been reached before their move. They would pay for meals and snacks prepared by Sister Colleen, and eat these in their designated dining cell. This suited both Sister Colleen who hated the thought of having people underfoot in her shrunken space, and the Kilgours who looked forward to the service.

At lunchtime, Hilma joined the Kilgours in keeping with her welcoming-tenants role.

"I suppose some of these renovations will be integrated into the retreat house area," said Dilly as she enjoyed a lunch of lentil soup, Greek salad and warm rolls.

"They will," said her husband who, as an official partner, was more involved than she with the overall planning. "That's why we invested in high quality appliances for the kitchenette and laundry."

"In time, there will be a sound system carrying chimes throughout the first and second floors to announce meal times and liturgical hours," said Hilma.

"But not on the third floor?"

"No. The condos are to be completely separate from the operation of the abbey," Graeme reminded her. "Once we move up there, our holiday is over."

"Daddy, you mean our camping," corrected Meri.

"Of course. Camping," said her father.

Lunch ended and Hilma helped the family carry their used dishes into the hall where a trolley had been set up for sorting dishes, cutlery, recyclables and trash. She explained that Sister Colleen would take it from there.

Back in their suite-of-rooms, Graeme and Dilly told the children it was time for their afternoon nap. So before taking her leave, Hilma put Gideon in the crib with his teddy bear. Tucking Meri into her nearby bed proved to be more challenging.

"I don't want a nap!" she protested. "I want to come with you."

"I have to go to work now," Hilma explained.

"I want Mommy!" yelled the child, trying to get out of her bed.

At the sound of the commotion, the child's mother entered the room. "You promised to help us with Gideon," she reminded her daughter.

"I'm four years old and fours don't have naps," said Meri.

"They do if they've been up early," said Dilly. "Read some books quietly until Gideon falls asleep."

Hilma quickly retrieved several books from where she'd stacked them on the dresser top and placed them on the bed beside Meri.

"When he falls asleep I'll get up," said the child.

"Fine," replied her mother.

"Are you having a nap?"

"I might."

"Is Daddy having a nap?"

"Daddy is still unloading our things."

"Then I want to help him."

"Later," said Dilly.

"I want Daddy to read me a story," pleaded the child.

"Daddy will read you a story tonight," said Dilly. "He's too busy right now."

"I don't like these books."

"You're testing me," said Dilly. "Not another word."

Midst tears and pouting, Meri flopped down with her pink blanket. Dilly ushered Hilma out of the room, closed the door and silently mouthed a *thank you*.

Hilma walked over to her office, a cell sandwiched between her music studio and the abbess' temporary office. A couple of weeks earlier, she'd been responsible for hiring movers to carry filing cabinets and book cases upstairs. The novices had helped transport computers, printers and basic supplies. The tiny office-cells were crowded but efficient.

Barely a half hour had passed when there was a knock on Hilma's office door and Graeme stuck his head in.

"Have you seen Meri?" he asked.

"No, is she missing?" asked Hilma, jumping up from her desk.

"I peeked in to see if the children were asleep and found Meri's bed empty," said Graeme. "She wasn't with Dilly either, so I thought she might be off looking for you."

"Have you checked with the sisters?" asked the abbess, stepping into the hall.

"Not yet," said Graeme. "I didn't want to be a complete nuisance on our first day here."

"I'll come with you," said Hilma, hurrying down the hall towards the nuns' quarters.

The child, however, was not with the sisters or Eula. Soon everyone was going cell to cell searching for her. When they were satisfied that Meri was not on the second floor, Dilly, Graeme and Hilma ran up the stairs to the third floor. With pounding hearts, they checked every cell, nook and cranny, calling her name. No Meri. Construction workers on the main floor had not seen her either.

"Could she have gone outside?" wondered the abbess.

The suggestion set off a stampede through the new side door. They raced out to the meadow and to their relief, found the little girl picking wildflowers in the meadow. Her pink blanket lay nearby.

"Meri, you are not to go out by yourself," scolded her father.

"I was with the girls," said the child, looking around as if for her absent playmates.

"There are no little girls here except you," her mother pointed out.

"Not *little* girls, Mommy! Big girls," said the child. "And a baby."

Twelve

Hilma was settling into a routine of office work and gardening, interspersed with occasional errands into town. She was now on a first name basis with the Black Springs librarian, postmaster and municipal clerk.

Along with all this, Sister Beatrice was almost tyrannical about her responsibility to instruct the young woman in the mastery of the chapel pipe organ. Hilma wondered if she was doing this solely to humour the abbess.

After a month of lessons, Hilma was feeling more competent on the instrument as well as more relaxed with the instructor. The nun was less unpleasant than she had originally feared, and although she was critical and short on praise, Hilma occasionally saw a softer side.

She had progressed considerably from the first day the nun had introduced her to manuals and stops. On that beginning day, Hilma had intently watched the master teacher demonstrate how stops provided voice, colour and pitch to the notes played on the manuals. There were four families of stops: principles, flutes, strings and reeds.

"What do you think?" asked Sister Beatrice.

"I love the way one instrument can create the sound of an entire orchestra," said Hilma, adding, "I hope I don't disappoint you." *Why am I being so obsequious?* thought Hilma, annoyed at herself. *This woman brings out all my insecurities.*

"We'll see," replied the nun, her eyes challenging and unsmiling.

It was all Hilma could do to stop herself from walking away in tears.

That same day, she learned that the chapel organ had four manuals, three to be played with one's hands. The fourth, known as the pedal board, was laid out in a keyboard arrangement for the feet. She was shown how the *Swell* manual has shutters allowing for varying dynamics of soft, loud and swells and that the *Great* is the manual used most often.

By the third week, Hilma could tell that the old organist was begrudgingly pleased with her progress.

"There's hope for you," the nun acknowledged. "Proficiency in your other instruments appears to be a bonus."

Hilma nodded in acknowledgement of the nun's off-handed compliment. She knew that the organist, and everyone else, could hear her music drifting through the second-floor halls whenever she played her beloved harp or cello.

However, concealing her gratification at these rare words of praise, Hilma returned the tribute. "The organ is a complex instrument," she said. "Even controlling volume is challenging, and you make it seem easy."

"It takes a skilled organist to play at three or four different volumes with hands and feet and fingers," said Sister Beatrice smugly. "Someday you'll be there."

Guess praise is over for the day, thought Hilma.

The chapel was the only room on the main floor to which the sisters and Hilma had access. When the contractors had dared suggest that the sisters confine their prayers to the second floor, Sister Beatrice had informed them that access to the pipe organ was critical both to liturgy and the advancement of her pupil.

And so one day in late July, ignoring the raised eyebrows and sighs of the builders, teacher and student made another of their regular treks from the back stairs through the construction zone to the chapel.

"What are you playing for me today?" asked the organist when Hilma was seated at the instrument and she beside her on a straight-backed chair.

"I'd like to begin with Handel's *Largo in G from Xerxes* and follow it with Bach's *A Minor Prelude and Fugue*."

The nun nodded and sat back to listen and watch.

Fingers flying over the keys, Hilma soon lost herself in the genius of Georg Friedrich Handel and Johann Sebastian Bach. Only a Senso could possibly master a new instrument that readily.

If Sister Beatrice was impressed, she hid it well. "Good," she said, at the conclusion of both works. "The pedalling was especially well executed. Could you play the middle section of the Fugue again with more bass emphasis?"

While playing the exercise dictated by the organist, Hilma felt a new presence in the chapel. Beneath one of the chapel's stain glass windows, a girl was listening to the music, sunlight tracing ribbons of colour through her hair. Her face was lifted in rapture.

"What is it?" asked Sister Beatrice, following her student's gaze.

"It's the girl with long brown hair," said Hilma without thinking. "She seems to be enjoying the music."

"What are you talking about?" asked the nun.

Hilma decided to divulge her secret. "I've been seeing girls around the abbey. I saw one in the cemetery with short fair hair and one in the meadow who had short dark hair and was carrying a baby. This is the one who has long brown hair. She was on the third floor landing the day I moved in."

"I don't see her, said the nun, looking about.

"She's gone now," said Hilma. "She faded away."

"And you say she was enjoying the music?"

"Totally absorbed in it," said Hilma.

Hilma noticed that the nun's face had blanched and that her eyes were bright with unshed tears. *I should never have told her,* she thought in dismay.

But Sister Beatrice surprised her. "Is seeing spirits one of your special abilities?" she asked.

"It's only recently I've been able to see them. It must have something to do with my year in Vapourlea."

"We prayed for you when you were missing," said the nun. "Your grandparents were distraught, you know."

"So you know about sensointuitive people?"

"Not a lot," replied the nun. "I know that there are families in the area that have this gene and that yours is one of them. Our abbess also has family members with the gene, Garth being one."

"What about the abbess herself?"

"She claims to have been skipped over, but we've always said that she has eyes in the back of her head."

"Do you know the girl I described?" asked Hilma.

"There was a girl here years ago who could fit the description. Myra was so musically talented that she was permitted to play the organ for liturgies in lieu of doing housekeeping tasks. She begged for lessons and I did give her some."

"What about the girl with short dark hair?"

"Shortly after Myra's own baby was given up for adoption, Corinne arrived here. The two became fast friends although they were very different. Corinne had short dark hair, but so did many girls."

"And the one I've seen with fair hair?"

"I'm not sure."

Sister Beatrice went on to describe how Corinne was always getting into trouble and Myra was forever making excuses for her. Corinne's baby was born about two weeks before Myra was to graduate from the year-long abbey program. Corinne was adamant about keeping the baby.

One night, two of the other penitents reported that they saw Corinne remove her baby from the nursery and leave by the back stairs. They woke Myra who ran after her. Neither the girls nor the baby were seen again.

"I could never understand Myra leaving that way," concluded the nun. "Corinne maybe, but not Myra."

"Do you have any idea what happened to them?" asked Hilma.

"I hoped they'd make decent lives for themselves somewhere."

"Did any other girls disappear?" asked Hilma.

"Through the years, there were a few girls who ran away rather than complete the year of training following the delivery. I suppose your fair-haired girl could be one of them."

"Did you not follow up on their disappearances?"

"Of course we did. Most girls found their way back to their families and the police were notified of any who didn't. Some of these girls had been disowned by their families so it didn't seem surprising for them to strike off on their own."

"Why am I seeing spirits at the abbey?"

"That I don't know," said Sister Beatrice, rising abruptly. "You can stay and practice if you wish."

At the door, she paused. "Hilma," she said in a stage whisper.

"Yes, Sister?"

"Don't breathe a word of this to Mother Abbess."

Hilma nodded uncertainly.

After the organist left the chapel, she tried to practice, but found herself too distracted to continue.

Thirteen

A week after the Kilgours had moved into their abbey cells, Garth Mayberry and his dog, Shadow, moved in two doors down from them.

"Are you sure you don't want two cells?" the abbess asked her great-nephew.

"One is perfect," Garth assured her. "Especially when the accommodations include laundry facilities, television and a café."

"The package doesn't include housekeeping services, though," teased Hilma, present in her professional capacity.

"I've been on my own for a long time and I'm very proficient at tidying up," he said. "Well, sort of."

"Can we leave you to move your belongings in?" asked the abbess. "Hilma and I will be in our offices if you need anything.

He assured his great-aunt that he would be fine, adding with a smile in Hilma's direction, that he knew where to find them.

Hilma followed the abbess down the hall, hoping she would not glance back at her blushing face, and promising herself that she would not be distracted by the police constable's proximity.

A few days later, the humane society phoned the abbey to inform the sisters that a two-year-old female border collie was available for adoption. Hilma took the call and passed the message on to the abbess.

"With all the other activity around here, I'd forgotten about that," said the abbess. "After our old dog died, Sister Helen pestered me until I gave her permission to phone in a request for a rescue dog."

The nuns consulted among themselves over lunch on whether they should wait until they were again living on the ground floor to take on a new pet.

"That particular dog will not wait till then," said Sister Helen.

"There will always be other dogs," said the abbess.

"I could free Hilma up from some of her gardening duties to become dog handler," persisted the porter. "She already minds Shadow when Garth's at work."

"Hilma doesn't only do gardening, you know," said Sister Beatrice. "She has other things to do."

"Hilma spends a lot of time with me," countered Sister Helen.

The abbess sighed but refrained from comment.

"Why don't we drive out to the shelter and take a look at the dog?" suggested Sister Martha who was home that day preparing for a case. "I could use a break."

Thus it came about that immediately after lunch, Sister Helen and Hilma accompanied Sister Martha to the shelter in the lawyer's Jetta.

At the shelter, the women followed an attendant along a row of large wire enclosures filled with barking dogs clamouring for attention. The man stopped before a cage that appeared empty.

"The border collie's in there," he said. "You'll see her at the back of the pen."

The women peered into the cage to find a black and white dog huddled in a corner, its dark eyes watching them fearfully.

"What's wrong with her?" asked Sister Martha.

"Puppy mill," said the attendant by way of explanation. "She'd already had two litters when she was rescued." He went on to describe what a mess she was when she arrived at the shelter, fur matted with feces, and paw pads raw from confinement in a cage with a wire grilled floor.

"Poor thing," said Sister Helen.

"Do you think she'll tolerate life at Black Springs Abbey?" wondered Sister Martha. "There's a lot of noise and commotion there now."

"Why don't you take her for a two-week trial period," suggested the attendant. "Then if she works out, you can proceed with immunization and spaying."

"She's very pretty," said Sister Helen. "Does she have a name?"

"We've been calling her Princess," said the man.

"Her name should be Daisy," said Hilma with conviction, crouching down to speak softly to the cowering animal.

"Any reason?" asked Sister Helen.

"She reminds me of a wildflower," replied Hilma.

"If you say so," said Sister Martha.

"It's perfect!" exclaimed Sister Helen.

"Come, Daisy," Hilma coaxed the frightened dog.

Trembling, the dog crawled slowly towards her. When it reached the front of the pen, it sniffed her fingers through the wire and whimpered. The attendant opened the door and attached a leash to the dog's collar. Cautiously, the animal inched through the opening and pressed itself against Hilma's legs.

"We have to take her with us," pleaded Hilma.

"Two week trial," insisted Sister Martha.

As soon as they returned to the abbey, Hilma took Daisy for a walk through the back fields. Initially, the dog hesitated to leave the smooth lawn for longer grasses. But soon it trotted at Hilma's side with growing confidence.

"You've never run free, have you?" she asked the dog. "As soon as you know that this is really your home, you won't need a leash."

She continued to talk to the dog and from time to time its tail gave a tentative wag. The woman and dog were returning to the abbey when unexpectedly they came across Claude sitting in the grass, his back against a jack pump.

Hilma jumped back startled and Daisy began to tremble.

The retired groundskeeper rose to his feet. "Where'd you get the dog?" he asked.

"The shelter."

"The nuns must have really taken to you, giving you a dog so soon."

"Daisy belongs to the sisters."

"Is dog walking one of your new jobs?" he asked

Hilma nodded.

"I love this place so much," said the man sadly.

"Were you here visiting Sister Helen?"

"I talked to her for a few minutes. Then she sent me on my way. You can see that I haven't gone very far yet," he added apologetically.

"Guess it's hard to adjust to retirement at first," sympathized Hilma.

"I don't know why the sisters let me go. I'm still in my prime," he said.

"The abbess said you have arthritis."

"I'm a bit stiff," conceded Claude. "But working around out here always loosened me up."

Seeing that the man would be happy to talk indefinitely, Hilma told him she had to get back to work. As she neared the abbey, Garth came through the new side door, Shadow at his side.

"Decided to come home for lunch," he explained. "This the new dog?"

"Her name is Daisy," said Hilma as the dogs sniffed each other and wagged their tails in greeting.

"Checking out your abbey investment, Constable?" asked Claude, walking over.

"Hello, Claude," said Garth, turning towards the man. "More than checking. I live here now."

"Really?"

"Moved in a few days ago."

"Beautiful dog there."

Thanks. His name is Shadow," said Garth.

Leaving the men to chat, Hilma walked Daisy to the cloister gate.

"Wait, Hilma," Garth called after her. "Let's exercise the dogs together."

"I guess I have a few minutes," said Hilma.

"Well, I'll be off then," said Claude, shifting from one foot to the other but making no real move to leave. "Anytime you need help just let me know."

"Sure thing, Claude. Enjoy the day," said Garth.

"Seemed reluctant to leave," said Hilma when the man was out of earshot.

"Probably finds time long on his hands," said Garth.

Out in the meadow, Garth picked up a stick and threw it for Shadow to retrieve. The dog bounded off and returned shortly, the stick firmly in his mouth. He danced about joyfully, mouth open, eyes begging for the game to resume.

"Let Daisy off her leash so she can chase too," he told Hilma.

"What if she runs away?"

"It's unlikely she will when she has a playmate."

As soon as Hilma unleashed Daisy, Garth hurled the stick high in the air. Shadow excitedly tore after it and, caught up in the moment, Daisy took a brief run before returning uncertainly to Hilma.

"She wants to play," observed Garth. "Just needs some practice."

"Guess she won't run away after all," said Hilma, patting the dog reassuringly.

"Just think," said Garth. "The dogs are playmates and you and I are housemates. Can you handle it?"

"I'll try," said Hilma. *I'll try not to break your heart.*

Fourteen

On the second week of August, XT and Azur moved to the abbey with their two-month-old daughters, Vi and Sarah. They had reached the decision to move only two days previously, prompted by the dread of realtors and potential buyers traipsing through their house.

"I was overwhelmed by the thought of keeping the place neat and spotless for showing, when all I wanted to do was catch up on lost sleep," explained Azur to Dilly and Hilma later that morning.

"I totally understand that," sympathized Dilly. "Babies don't seem to empathize with sleep-deprived parents."

"That's why babies come with innate cuteness," laughed Azur.

"Whose idea was it to move here so suddenly?"

"XT's, if you can believe," said Azur. "Knowing how stressed I was about the house-selling ordeal, he announced that he had an idea he was almost afraid to run by me. I told him to go ahead since the suspense was killing me."

"And so he said…"

"He said, 'What about moving to the abbey with the others and leaving our house in a permanent state of spotless neatness for the realtors?'" Azur quoted her husband.

"Like Garth did," said Dilly.

"Except that Garth put his furniture in storage, whereas XT insisted we leave our furniture behind until we move into our condo."

"That makes sense," said Dilly, approvingly. "Even if the house sells quickly, many buyers count on a delay for financing."

"Needless to say, I told him I found the notion definitely appealing, so he discussed it with the Abbess," Azur continued.

"I saw him here with Abbess and thought they were discussing business," said Dilly.

"They were," said Azur.

"You could have asked me," said Hilma smugly.

"Come to think of it, why didn't you tell me your sister was moving here, Miss Business Manager?" asked Dilly.

"I wanted her to tell you herself."

Dilly patted Hilma's arm forgivingly. "So what happened after XT talked to Abbess?" she prompted.

Azur described how her husband returned from the abbey and announced they would be staying on the same corridor as Garth and the Kilgours. They hastily packed clothing and supplies for the move, knowing that they could return to their house as needed for other necessities.

"Your cells are nearest the construction area," Hilma noted, "but it's all blocked off and safe."

"We only have two cells and it'll be a bit noisy," said Azur, "but I'm not complaining."

"Not much noisier than it is for all of us," said Dilly. "And don't forget the real bonus."

"Which is…"

"Having all our meals prepared for us."

"Oh yes. That was the clincher," admitted Azur.

"You'll be sharing a dining cell with Garth, but you'll have your own tub room and toilet," said Hilma.

"Guys, I said I'm not complaining. Look, one of our cells even has a sink and towel rack."

"Is XT's brother still coming next week?" asked Dilly.

"He is," said Azur. "We put the crib in our room so Ethan can have the other one to himself."

XT's parents were going on a two-week Mediterranean cruise and their autistic son, Ethan, could not be left unattended. It was Azur who, several months earlier, had extended the invitation to the young man. At the time, XT's mother, Sarah, had questioned the timing of the visit. But Azur reasoned that, since she would be on maternity leave, it was actually the perfect time. Moving to the abbey had not been in the equation at the time.

"It's a good thing the babies are in a single crib," said Dilly.

"Yes, we're not going to use the second crib until we move into the condo," said Azur. "They'll think sleeping together is the norm until we move upstairs."

"They mightn't like the two-crib norm when the time comes," said Hilma.

"Probably not at first," said Azur, laughing.

Lying together in their crib, the twins began to fuss. Azur announced that it was feeding time and Dilly excused herself to check on her own children who were supposedly resting.

Azur picked up Sarah, changed her diaper and handed her over to Hilma while she turned her attention to Vi. With both babies changed, she began to breast feed them.

"Is it hard breast feeding them both at once?" asked Hilma.

"It's twice as fast as feeding them individually, and easier than bottle feeding," replied Azur.

Happy to have her sister to herself, Hilma began to open boxes piled in the hallway and put clothing in drawers and closets. Equally glad for the assistance, Azur told her to put things wherever she thought they would fit. She would rearrange them at her leisure.

When the twins were fed, Azur returned them to the crib where they chuckled and cooed to each other.

"I'm going to let Shadow out of Garth's room and take Daisy and him out for a run," said Hilma. "On my way up, I'll be bringing garden vegetables to the kitchenette. Sister Helen finds it tiring to go up and down the stairs."

Before Hilma could leave, Meri and Gideon burst into the room and rushed over to the crib.

"Hi baby!" said Gideon loudly.

"Don't wake the babies," shouted Meri.

"No sleep," noted her brother.

"Children, what are you doing?" asked Dilly arriving on the scene to find Gideon scaling the crib and Meri stroking one of the little heads.

"You are not to touch the babies without permission," she admonished, extracting Gideon from the crib bars.

Sarah was now wailing loudly while her sister, Vi, was whimpering in sympathy. Sighing, Azur picked up her daughters and placed them, still crying, on the nearby bed.

"Put them in a playpen," instructed Meri.

"They don't have a playpen yet," said Azur testily. "They were fine before you upset them with all the noise."

"We'd better go back to our rooms, children," said Dilly curtly, taking Gideon's hand.

"No! No!" screamed Meri. "I want to stay."

"Actually, you can stay," said Azur, recovering from her lapse of patience. "It momentarily slipped my mind that I'm the adult in this scenario."

"Motherhood generates a protective instinct," said Dilly, accepting the off-handed apology. "Meri and Gideon may have been a bit rambunctious but somehow we need to work out a team approach — at least while we're living together on this floor."

"I'm not sure what you mean by *team approach*," said Azur.

"Sort of like a co-op nursery," said Dilly. "We can do all sorts of things together and also spell each other off for breaks."

While their mother prattled happily on, Meri and Gideon climbed onto the bed beside the twins. Unperturbed by the babies' fussing, Meri exuberantly kissed Vi's tiny hands and Gideon began exploring Sarah's nose with his chubby finger.

Hilma looked on anxiously, waiting for her sister's reaction.

"You know, Dillian," said Azur, "two babies are quite enough for me to manage at this time. I would be more interested in seeing a few house rules put in place than in a co-op arrangement."

There was a strained nonchalance in Azur's voice while a look of disbelief crossed Dilly's face. Hilma figured it was a good time to attend to her tasks.

"I'll be around," she said, slipping away.

Fifteen

XT met Ethan at the London airport and watched with his brother as their parents boarded an Air Canada flight. As they waited, the brothers talked.

"Dad and Mom left their car in the airport parking lot to fly to Toronto and Athens," typed Ethan on his Mini iPad. The device was his voice and indeed did talk when he pressed the *Speak* button.

"They're going to have a great time," said XT, "and so are you."

"They have gone on a Mediterranean Cruise and my vacation is at Black Springs Abbey."

"We'll all be having a great time," said XT.

"Yes," replied Ethan. "They will be safe on the plane and the cruise ship."

"They will be *very* safe," XT said, knowing how much regular reassurance the autistic man needed.

"We're going to your new apartment in the abbey," typed Ethan.

"It's more like a hotel," explained XT. "We have our own rooms and we share meals with the others who live there."

"Who lives there?"

XT listed off the names of all the people living on the second floor of Black Springs Abbey.

"That sounds like too many people," said Ethan.

"You won't be seeing them all at once. They'll be doing their own thing, going to work or being inside their own rooms. You'll have your own room too."

"Where is my room?"

"Right beside ours," said XT. "Oh, look. There they go!" The airplane coasted slowly down the runway, picked up speed and soared off into the clear blue sky.

Only when the plane was no longer visible did Ethan pick up his duffle bag and accompany his brother to the neurologist's parked car.

By the third day of his stay at the abbey, Ethan had settled into a reassuring routine. His day began with breakfast in one of the small dining rooms in the company of XT, Azur and Garth. Unless Sarah and Vi were sleeping, they were also there in their stroller.

"How are things going?" Garth asked him.

"Good, now that Daisy sleeps in my room," typed Ethan.

Twice during his first night at the abbey, Ethan had entered XT and Azur's room and wakened them with his anxious pacing. Bleary-eyed the following morning, XT was glad that he had booked himself off work for the duration of his brother's visit.

It was then Hilma suggested to Ethan that Daisy become his companion dog. She told him that Shadow spent the night in Garth's room and Daisy would be happy to sleep in his. Ethan wondered where she usually slept and was told that she had a bed in the back hallway where the sisters lived. Next he worried that the sisters would mind if he borrowed their dog.

In response, Hilma retrieved Sister Helen who told him it would be an honour for Daisy to be his service dog. And so the abbey dog was recruited to be Ethan's guardian for the duration of his stay. For his part, Ethan took over Hilma's dog-walking role.

"I hope the dogs are behaving themselves for you," said Garth.

"Yes, they run around outside but they never run away," said Ethan.

Mid-morning the man went to his room to play Solitaire and Mahjongg on his iPad. He left the door open so that Shadow and Daisy could enter if they wished. However, the visitor who entered his room was not canine but four-year-old Meri.

"What are you doing?" she asked him.

Ethan remained intent on his iPad game.

"What are you doing, Ethan?" she repeated.

He looked at the child but did not reply. Typing on the device would require switching from his game.

"Hi, Ethan," said Dilly, coming to retrieve her daughter. "Would you like to come with me and the children in half an hour to do some painting?"

"Yes," he replied verbally in his guttural voice.

And thus his daily routine expanded. Dilly had set up a makeshift studio in the empty cell between Garth's and theirs, and under the artist's supervision, Ethan, Meri and Gideon created acrylic abstracts.

After joining his brother's family for lunch, Ethan took Daisy and Shadow for a walk around the abbey property. With XT discretely watching his brother from a distance, Ethan and the dogs stopped to observe construction workers engaged in their renovation projects, inspected some of the old sheds and examined the workings of a pump jack.

"Would you like to take Sarah and Vi for a stroller ride?" suggested Azur when the men and dogs returned to the floor.

Obligingly, Ethan pushed the twins up and down the corridor until Meri tried to help him.

"No!" he said, pulling away and rushing the stroller back to Azur. When she asked him if there was a problem, all he could do was look distressed and flap his hands.

Vi and Sarah, however, were delighted with their speedy ride down the corridor and chortled in delight.

"Maybe you can put the babies in their playpen and let them play," said Azur.

Awkwardly, the man transferred the squirming babies from stroller to playpen where they began to cry in protest. Ethan became increasingly disturbed, angst etched on his face.

"Go get your iPad and tell us what's wrong," said XT.

"Meri pushed the babies and it was my job," he typed. "Now they're crying."

Relieved that the issue was a minor one, Azur and XT explained to him that Meri was merely acting like any little girl. Mollified by the explanation, Ethan agreed to go to his room and listen to music through his head phones.

Later he accompanied Hilma on a shopping trip into town in the abbey's dark green Ford F-150 pickup.

"Do you like my truck, Ethan?" she asked him.

Ethan nodded.

"It really belongs to the abbey but it's mine now because I'm the errand girl. I used to drive Bram's car sometimes, but I've never had my own vehicle before."

After Hilma and Ethan returned some books to the library and picked up some building forms at the Municipal offices, they treated themselves to ice cream cones in the Black Springs variety store.

Following the evening meal, Ethan watched the news with Hilma and Eula until it was time to take the dogs out for their final run of the day. He retired to his room early and listened to music on his iPad while Daisy curled up contentedly on her dog bed.

With the twins asleep and Ethan wanting time alone, XT and Azur joined Hilma, Garth, Graeme and Dilly in the entertainment room.

"Aren't baby monitors a blessing!" said Dilly, setting her monitor on the table beside that of the Moonstorey-Barkleys.

"I'll say!" replied Azur. "I wouldn't be able to tear myself away from them otherwise."

"How are things going with Ethan?" asked Graeme.

"Really well," said XT. "As long as he has a routine to follow, he's fine."

"It's nice of you to include him in your painting classes, Dilly," said Azur.

"The children enjoy having him around. Speaking of whom, I'm glad you took me to task about the children's behaviour," said Dilly.

"Hope I wasn't too rough," said Azur.

"I was hurt at the time. After all Meri and Gideon are *my* babies. But making a few simple rules for them to follow has made all our lives easier."

"I have to admit we found their little tantrums and demands amusing until we made ourselves see their behaviour as others might," said Graeme. "Meri's our little princess and Gideon is our pint-sized entertainer. We thought everyone saw them that way."

"Respecting people's privacy and touching babies only with permission are two new rules we've been practicing," said Dilly.

"They're doing very well considering the number of nooks and crannies on this floor for little people to want to explore," said Azur.

"You know, Ethan's need for routine is also providing a useful model for us," said Dilly.

"For all of us," agreed Azur. "It would be tempting to let the twins continue sleeping in our room after Ethan leaves. But getting Vi and Sarah accustomed to sleeping by themselves is a routine they may as well learn right away."

"Routine can be reassuring," said Hilma pensively.

"Hey, Garth, I notice you're not contributing to this conversation," said Graeme.

"My range of experience doesn't include family matters," he replied.

Hilma detected a rueful tone in his voice and fixed her attention on the television screen, blocking his senso efforts to reach out to her.

Sixteen

On a humid day in late August, Hilma was in the garden alone, Sister Helen being in bed with a virus. Her gardening task for the day was to dig up carrots and parsnips for dinner. Shaking the dirt from the roots as she unearthed them, she placed them in a bucket for Sister Colleen.

Having grown accustomed to workmen coming and going around the abbey, she paid little attention to the creak of the gate swinging open and shut or to the sound of footsteps upon the pebbled walk.

However, sensing someone standing behind her, she turned to see who had approached so close and was startled to find Claude watching her.

"Sorry, I didn't mean to frighten you," he said.

"Sister Helen's not here," said Hilma.

"Where is she?"

"She's not feeling well."

Claude shuffled around indecisively, reluctant to leave as Hilma continued to dig up the vegetables and drop them into the bucket.

"Here, let me help you," he said, crouching down to pull up a stubborn parsnip root.

"It's okay, Claude," said Hilma. "I prefer to work alone. Thanks, though, for offering to help."

"You can't imagine how it feels to be unwanted and useless," he said morosely, brushing bits of earth from his hands as he rose to his feet.

"You probably need more time to adjust to retirement," she said. "You're accustomed to being busy."

"I'm certainly not used to spending my time playing bingo or shuffleboard or doing exercises with a bunch of old fogies."

Hilma thought there could be worse fates for an elderly man, but she remained silent.

"I hate people telling me what I should be doing: 'Claude, there's a choir coming to sing for us this afternoon.' 'Claude, did you know there's a movie tonight?'"

"Do they *make* you participate?" she asked.

"Not exactly, but they get on my nerves, always reminding me what's on the recreation calendar. Like I can't read," he said derisively.

"Are there things you can do on your own?"

"Sure. I can sit in my room staring out the window."

Hilma pulled a few more vegetables and leaned her hoe against the wall. She wiped the back of her gloved hand against her brow and picked up the basket of parsnips and carrots.

"Can I carry that for you?" offered Claude.

"Thanks, but I'm fine."

"I always thought I'd live out my life on abbey property," said Claude. "That's why I keep coming here. It's a good thing I can still drive my old Chevy."

"I have to take these in now, Claude. Sister Colleen is waiting for me."

"Seems people are always waiting for you."

"Are they?" she asked.

"You were gone a whole year before your sister brought you back. People wondered where you were."

"What are you saying?" she asked, taken aback.

"You're one of those Sensos, aren't you?" he asked.

Hilma's mouth opened but no words came out.

"It's okay, Hilma. You can trust me."

"Where is this conversation going?" asked Hilma, finding her voice.

"I just know what folks hereabouts say. They used to call your grandmother a witch, you know, but the sisters liked her and that was good enough for me."

"Why are you talking about Sensos and my grandmother?" asked Hilma.

"Please, don't be mad at me. I shouldn't have said anything. It's just that you seem so lost and lonely. I feel the same way and I thought we could be friends."

"You don't know me at all," said Hilma.

It was then the cloister gate swung open, this time to admit XT, Ethan and the dogs.

"Visiting again, Claude?" asked the physician.

"I keep hoping someone here needs me."

"I think we're doing fine," said XT.

"Well, I'll be on my way then. I've enjoyed talking to you, Hilma," said Claude.

He slipped through the gate and was gone.

"You have no idea how happy I am to see you guys," said Hilma, setting down the bucket she had been clutching. She was close to tears and wondered if she was upset because Claude had spoken the truth in describing her as lost and lonely or if she was annoyed at his unsolicited familiarity.

"What does that old man know about me?" she muttered.

"Was Claude bothering you?" asked XT.

Hilma told her brother-in-law what the man had said about Mavis, and how he had talked about her year-long absence from Creekside.

"I'll speak to the abbess about him," he said.

"XT, do you think I'm lost and lonely?"

"Do you feel that you are?"

Hilma contemplated the question. Surrounded as she was by people who loved her, why *would* she feel that way?

"I feel as if my heart were yearning for something," she finally said.

"Listen to your heart," said XT.

★ ★ ★

By mid-morning the following day, Hilma had already delivered several baskets of butternut and acorn squash to Sister Colleen on the second floor. The cook, a whirlwind of peeling, chopping, blanching and cooling, was freezing squash. She was determined to not let inconveniences caused by renovations interfere with canning, pickling and freezing the abbey's fruits and vegetables for the coming winter.

Thus, on many days throughout the summer, pots of jams, sauces and preserves of every kind simmered aromatically on the range top. Bowls, spoons, tongs, strainers and empty jars shared space with filled jars cooling on racks atop a long table which occupied the middle of the kitchenette.

"Does it look like there's room for more bodies in this cramped space?" she retorted whenever Sisters Fazeela and Jamini offered to help her. Consciences appeased, the novices slipped away to their regular tasks.

Sister Helen, having recovered from her summer ailment, was overseeing Hilma's selection of gourds.

"We have a good crop of them this year," she said with satisfaction, admiring the sprawling vines heavy with butternut, acorn, spaghetti and pepper squash as well as pumpkins.

Carrying up her final basket-full of squash for the morning, Hilma passed Ethan heading down, the dogs on his heels.

"I'll join you in a few minutes," she told him.

Ethan gave her a quick glance of acknowledgement, but by the time she exited the side doorway, there was no sign of the man and dogs. Ethan and the dogs had become quite the adventurers and she wondered where on the property they might be.

She might find them at the front of the abbey watching the builders or in the back meadow enjoying the marvels of nature. Then again, they could be walking the shaded flagstone paths laid out by the landscapers earlier in the summer.

Hilma found Ethan in the meadow, walking quickly through the tall grasses and wildflowers. Daisy and Shadow ran freely nearby.

"Ethan!" she called, running to catch up.

But Ethan continued to walk quickly away from her. It wasn't until she drew closer that she noticed he was following the fair-haired girl she had seen in the cemetery on her first day with Sister Helen. *Ethan can see her*, she thought in surprise.

The girl glanced over her shoulder at Hilma before fading away. Ethan came to an abrupt stop, looking about curiously.

"You saw the girl, didn't you?" she asked when she reached him.

Ethan looked puzzled.

"I need to talk to you about her," she said. "Can you run upstairs and bring down your iPad?"

Ethan continued to regard her questioningly.

"Please, Ethan. It's important."

Ethan left Hilma in the meadow with the dogs and went up to his room. He returned shortly with his communication device.

"Tell me about the girl," she said, standing at his side to read his response.

"What girl?" typed Ethan.

"The girl you were following," she said.

"I didn't see a girl," he said.

"But you hurried to catch up with her."

"I was following a white light."

"What do you mean?"

"It was wispy and bright."

"What do you think it was?" asked Hilma.

"It looked like an aura. Did you see it?" he typed, looking perplexed.

Hilma hesitated before replying. "I don't have the gift of seeing auras. I saw a spirit person."

"It's sad you don't see auras," said Ethan. "When I was a child, I thought everyone saw them, but now I know that most people don't."

"Do you often see auras?"

"Yes, everyone has one. Yours is pale blue with violet rays. It makes me feel good to be near you."

"What colour is your aura?"

"Azur tells me mine is green with rays of blue. Azur doesn't have autism but she still sees auras."

"Azur sees auras because she's sensointuitive," she told him. "Most Sensos see auras."

"You saw the spirit girl and I saw the white aura," he typed.

"Were you frightened?"

"Not frightened at all. It wanted me to follow."

With that, Ethan closed his iPad and they walked along companionably while the dogs romped and chased. It was satisfying to see Daisy's tail waving boldly rather than hanging pitifully between her hind legs. She had changed remarkably from the cowering animal retrieved from the shelter.

Unexpectedly, Ethan began walking with renewed determination through the meadow's tall grasses and wildflowers, setting off flurries of humming insects, buzzing bees and fluttering butterflies. Daisy and Shadow tussled briefly before racing after him.

Quickening her pace to keep up with them, Hilma stumbled over the dogs and almost bumped into Ethan when he came to an abrupt halt. Squatting down to inspect something on the meadow floor, he reached through the overgrowth to touch a large flat stone concealed by nature's relentless claim on the land.

"What is it?" she asked.

Ethan rose from his crouched position, opened his iPad and typed. "This is where the white light stopped."

Hilma bent over for a closer look.

"You've discovered the labyrinth," she told him.

Seventeen

At the end of the week, Jake and Evelyn Barkley arrived at Black Springs Abbey to pick up their son, Ethan. After they rang the bell at the cloister gate, Sister Helen ushered them into the garden and invited them to take a seat on a garden bench while she summoned him.

Within minutes, Ethan rushed down the back stairs carrying his luggage and iPad to greet them.

"I had a good time at the abbey but I'm ready to go home," he typed.

"Give your Dad and me a hug," said his mother, eliciting a rather wooden embrace, but satisfying them nonetheless.

Soon XT and Azur, each holding a baby joined them. The proud grandparents fussed over the dark-eyed twins they were seeing for the first time.

"I knew from their pictures they'd be beautiful, and they're totally gorgeous," said Evelyn.

"Sister Beatrice wants you to come to the chapel and listen to her star pupil, Hilma, play the organ for you," said XT.

"It will be good for Hilma to have you there because she needs practice performing in public," Azur told her in-laws.

Seated at the organ, Hilma smiled nervously at the small audience sitting in pews at the front of the lovely chapel. Sister Beatrice stood behind her, ready to turn pages.

The performer took a deep breath and began to play a stirring rendition of Bach's *Prelude and Fugue in G Minor* followed by a mystical performance of *Jesu, Joy of Man's Desiring*.

The audience applauded in genuine appreciation.

"She's been playing the organ for only two months," Azur proudly informed the Barkleys.

"Unbelievable!" said Jake Barkley.

"You should hear her play harp and cello," said XT.

"Sister Beatrice deserves all the credit," insisted Hilma, uncomfortable with the praise.

"I've never had a student like Hilma before," said the organist.

Hilma blushed and fidgeted with her hands.

It was then Ethan began to hum. Although he loved music and had been entranced by the organ recital, he was eager to be on his way.

"Young man, your behaviour is unacceptable," said Sister Beatrice, turning to him crossly.

Shocked by the organist's harsh tone of voice, Ethan jumped to his feet and faced his mother, flapping his hands. The Barkleys thanked the organist for the recital and excused themselves hastily from the chapel.

Embarrassed, the others followed as quickly as it seemed proper to do so.

"Really!" said Evelyn Barkley. "That nun is sadly lacking in empathy. I hope Ethan was able to steer clear of her during his time at the abbey."

"Sister Beatrice's bark is worse than her bite," said XT. "Wouldn't you agree, Hilma?"

"She can be quite intimidating, but she responds well to diligent effort," said Hilma.

"In other words, she responds well to her idea of perfection," said Azur. "Fortunately, Hilma possesses exceptional talent."

"And yet you encouraged me to enter the dragon's den," Hilma reminded her sister.

"I knew you had what it takes," said Azur with a smile.

By now Ethan had opened his iPad and was intently typing.

"Sister Beatrice scared me. I don't like her."

"Never mind, dear," said his mother. "You behaved very well during Hilma's recital. And I know you'll be fine at the Galvinstons'."

"Why are we going there?" he asked.

"Bram and Mavis have kindly invited us for dinner before we head home," said his father.

Ethan climbed into the back seat of his family's car with his luggage for the ride to the Galvinstons'. Hilma, who was going to the same place, rode in the back seat of XT's Volvo between the two baby car seats.

The Galvinston house on Warren Avenue stood on property that sloped down to Bear Creek at its back. It was a dignified white brick building with black shutters. Typical of the style known as Italianate Village, it had a low angled roof, boxed cornices with brackets and tall windows. Ornate gingerbread decorated the verandah which wrapped itself along the front and one side.

As the guests proceeded to the stately front door, they passed a charming lamppost surrounded by shrubs and flowers in the manicured front lawn.

Bram and Mavis greeted them at the entrance and welcomed them into their front hall which boasted a magnificent, winding stairway and opened onto a formal living room to the right.

"I remember the first time I was in this foyer five years ago," said XT. "Miss Azur Moonstorey, looking ravishing, took my breath away gliding down these stairs."

"Really?" asked his wife. "I remember *running* down them because I had so much to do that day."

"Now that I recall, you were rather aloof and dismissive."

"Could it be that I was a bit stressed and you were rather brash?"

"Apparently it all turned out well in the end," observed Jake.

While they awaited the dinner announcement, Bram guided his guests into the parlour, a cozy autumn-dappled sunroom decorated in tasteful antiques. Hilma followed Mavis into the kitchen to assist her grandmother put the finishing touches on dinner.

Soon they were called to the dining room where they took their places around a large oak table already set with goblets of ice water and steamy crockeries of roasted squash and apple cream soup. The remaining dishes were served family-style in large bowls containing spinach, broccoli, potatoes and roast chicken, all enhanced with Mavis' unique blends of herbs and nuts. Dessert was rhubarb pie served with coffee.

"This smells and looks amazing," said Jake. "I bet you don't eat like this at the abbey."

"There's nothing like my grandmother's cooking," agreed Hilma.

"I thought you said Sister Colleen was a good cook," Mavis reminded her.

"She's definitely above average, but you're the cookery queen," said Azur.

"You're a lucky man, XT, to have all these excellent cooks looking after you," Evelyn told her son.

In the course of the meal, conversation turned to the professional relationships shared by Evelyn's sister, Janet Tennyson, and her friend, Mavis Galvinston. Both sensointuitive healers, Janet had been a pharmacist during the time Mavis worked as a midwife. The same people who regarded their talents with wariness, rushed to them for help when they had health concerns.

As they were enjoying pie and coffee, an elegant feline with pale green eyes and a silvery blue coat entered the room and made its way purposefully toward XT. The cat rubbed against his leg, purring loudly.

"Bleu, you rascal, you still like me," said XT.

"You know very well she's obsessed with you," said Azur.

"What a lovely cat," said Evelyn Barkley.

Her physician son agreed, although he declined to relate to his parents how the cat's fur could take on a deep blue hue and her eyes became glowing sapphires when facing psychic vampires. Nor did he tell them that Bleu was a catalyst capable of enabling a non-sensointuitive person to cross into another dimension. Specifically, a person like Dr. Xavier Tennyson Barkley.

XT knew that, despite the sensointuitive gene on his mother's side of the family, Jake and Evelyn Barkley were largely unaware of all that could transpire through bearing such genetic makeup.

When it was time to leave, Ethan opened his iPad and thanked the Galvinstons for a delicious dinner. Then he went over to Hilma and typed, "Be careful, Hilma."

"Careful of what?" she asked.

"Danger at abbey."

Eighteen

In September, Graeme began teaching in the Math department at the Providence Crossing high school. He was assigned to instruct senior students in calculus and vectors, and junior students in the foundations of mathematics. After the first few days, he settled comfortably into his new routine, enjoying both students and co-workers.

Left to her own devices, Dilly wandered the abbey grounds with Meri and Gideon. They watched the builders engaged in their many tasks. They explored the meadow with its plethora of plants, insects and birds. They walked the gently twisting flagstone path through the wooded area at the property's front, and discussed the shadows laid out by young trees planted along the path's sunnier sections. They visited the chicken coop, browsed around decrepit sheds with sagging roofs and rotting timbers and circled a ramshackle cabin locked and shuttered.

One of the buildings drew Dilly back time and again, a small barn with a high stone foundation supporting weathered plank walls. The foundation had a door and two windows on one side. On the opposite side, a wide stone and earthen ramp led up to a large double door. Chunks of mortar had fallen from the foundation stones and sections of boards were missing from its battered walls.

Entering through the ground-level door one sunny morning, Dilly found herself in the lower of two levels. In the dim light provided by the grimy windows, she was able to make out a stone floor, an open central area, six large pens and a stairs leading to the upper floor.

"Mommy, can I come in?" called Meri.

"Stay with Gideon, sweetie. I'll be right out," said Dilly.

Taking a final quick look around, she could envision canvases drying against the walls, easels holding works in progress, shelves covered with paints, jars, brushes, blocks of clay and art tools. Here was a place for the potter's wheel currently stored in her mother's garage and the kiln she would buy.

As she came out squinting in the bright light, she found Claude standing beside the children.

"I see you've found the old goat barn," he said.

"Interesting old building," said Dilly.

"Yup. Seems like only yesterday it was full of goats and straw and milking equipment," said the man.

"Mommy wants to paint out here," said Meri.

"Does she now? It could be fixed up real nice for that," said Claude."

"I think so too," said Dilly. "But I've been told that workers won't get around to tackling any outbuildings until they're finished with the abbey. And that's going to be a long time."

"You're an artist, are you?"

"Yes, and I'd love to set up a studio."

"Good place for one."

"I want to explore the upper level with a flashlight sometime. Do you know what's up there?"

"Used to be for storing straw and hay for the goats. I wouldn't advise you going up there though. Floor could give. It should be reinforced before people start walking around on it."

"Oh," said Dilly, disappointed.

"Come around to the other side, though, and I'll show it to you off the ramp."

Dilly and the children followed Claude around the barn and climbed the ramp. They watched as Claude pulled on one of the wide doors and swung it open on creaking hinges. Beyond the door was a single large room extending the length of the barn, strands of straw thinly covering its floor.

"Kitty," said Gideon, pointing his finger into the semi-darkness.

"Yes, you'll find kitties up here, little lad. Mice and barn swallows too," said the old caretaker, tousling the boy's hair.

"Can we go in?" asked Meri.

"Better not," said Claude. "The floor was once solid enough to hold a horse and wagon, but I wouldn't trust it now."

"Horsey!" shouted Gideon.

"Where did the horse live?" asked Meri.

"In one of the sheds. It had a nice stall in there."

"So you wouldn't recommend putting a studio up here," said Dilly.

"Not to start with. Along with the floor problems, it doesn't have the weather protection provided by the thick stone walls below. Those walls kept the goats warm in winter and cool in summer."

"Where did you live when you were here, Claude?" asked Meri.

"I lived in a little room at the back of the abbey kitchen when I was a boy. Then I moved out to the cabin in my late teens."

"Oh, the little cabin by the sheds," said Dilly.

Claude nodded. "I used to keep it real nice. Now it has that gloomy abandoned look."

"An artist needs good lighting and this barn isn't hooked up to electricity," said Dilly, returning to the topic of her longed-for studio.

"It would be fairly simple to run a buried extension cord from the abbey. All you'd need's a heavy-duty cable plugged into a grounded house circuit."

"That sounds time consuming."

"Could be done in a day or two. I think you'd also need new windows. Modern windows would help with both light and insulation."

"I don't suppose I'll see any of this done for ages," sighed Dilly.

"If you buy the material and tell me what you want, I'd be happy to do the work," said Claude.

Dilly discussed the idea with Graeme and the others later that day. Almost everyone was in agreement that it could be a win–win arrangement: Dilly would get her studio and Claude would again feel useful, if only for a while.

"It would keep him from moaning around the cloister garden bothering Sister Helen and me," said Hilma.

"It would keep him from interfering with the novices whenever they mow the grass," said Sister Martha. "He keeps telling them they're going too fast or too slow on the lawn tractor, and offering to change the oil or sharpen the blades when they're quite capable of doing these things themselves."

"It's a terrible idea!" snapped Sister Beatrice, interrupting the positive flow in the conversation. "Claude needs to stay away from the abbey once and for all and make a new life for himself. This will only prolong the transition period. Don't you agree, Mother Abbess?"

Dilly held her breath.

"There's merit in what you're saying, Beatrice," said the abbess carefully. "On the other hand, this project would give the poor man something productive to do until the inclement weather of late fall and winter makes him more willing to stay indoors in his new residence," said the abbess.

"So I can go ahead and start planning?" asked Dilly, trying to contain her excitement.

Midst exclamations of encouragement and offers of help, the sole objector was the organist who tightened her mouth in disapproval and said nothing further.

★ ★ ★

In the weeks that followed, the goat barn was slowly rejuvenated. Dilly ordered the building supplies and materials requested by Claude. Hilma picked them up in the Ford.

Initially, there was a bit of fuss when Claude thought he should be the one driving the pickup during the building process. When Hilma complained about his interference, the abbess personally came outside to meet with him.

"It's Hilma's job now to look after business matters," the abbess told him.

"But I know the locations of the lumber yards and hardware stores," protested Claude. "Besides, I can check that the orders are correct."

"Hilma needs to learn such things," said the abbess.

"She's not strong enough to lift heavy planks and boxes and cans and stuff."

"Large orders are always delivered directly by the companies involved. As for smaller lots of merchandise, the salespeople can load the pickup for Hilma at their end. You can unload it when it gets here, Claude. The pickup belongs to Hilma now and you are not to drive it."

"Perhaps I'll just accompany her then to make sure they give her the right products," said Claude.

"That will not be necessary," said the abbess firmly, holding his gaze until he looked away. Since her word was law here, the matter was not discussed again.

In no time, electricity was installed in the barn and Claude installed lighting throughout the lower level. Next, he replaced the old barn windows with modern triple-pane ones. To move things along, Graeme and Garth spent their off-work time covering the stone floor with insulation board and maple flooring.

Given the go-ahead to do some inside painting, Dilly painted the stone walls a pale cream colour, then sanded and stained the woodwork to match the rich hues of the maple floor.

Throughout this time, Claude worked relentlessly away on the outside of the building. He repaired chipped mortar in the stonework, replaced missing timber in the barn walls and patched the roof. He more than earned the hourly rate paid him by Dilly.

"The doors should be replaced," he told Dilly at one point.

"New doors will be included in the renovations we do on the barn at a later date," she said. "Once I start giving lessons, I'll want a washroom on the upper level as well as a little shop."

"So you'd be allowing outsiders on the property," he said. Dilly detected disapproval in his voice.

"I shouldn't think many people will be coming," she said. "Possibly people coming here on retreat and artists wanting art supplies."

One day Graeme came home from school to tell his wife that he'd learned of students looking for co-op placements. He wondered if she could use such a student.

"Would painting the outside of the barn be within the parameters of such a placement?" she asked him.

A day later, Graeme reported back that Mason Ibbetson, the shop teacher, wanted to assign not one, but two students to Dilly's barn painting project. Their names were Clark Miller and Jackson Kelly, and for the duration of the semester, they could work from eight to eleven each weekday morning. Both boys lived in Black Springs and would drive to the abbey in Jackson's car. Dilly would be responsible for their safety and supervision as well as for submitting weekly reports to the school.

Dilly readily accepted. Azur, because she was on maternity leave, was able to keep Gideon and Meri occupied during the time her friend was with the students. Hilma shopped for the brushes, rollers and paint Dilly requested, and Claude put up the scaffolding.

"I know why you chose grey paint, Mrs. Kilgour," said Jackson on the second day of his placement.

"You do?"

"It's because the barn wants to keep its weathered look."

"The *barn* does?" asked Dilly, amused.

"I understand these things because I'm like you," said Jackson.

Really?" asked Dilly.

"You can trust both of us, Mrs. Kilgour," said Clark. "Jackson's a Senso like you and I've been his friend forever, even though I'm not one. We were excited when this co-op placement came up because we want to talk to you about the train."

"The train?" asked Dilly.

"The Hallowmas train," said Jackson.

"Have you seen this train?" asked Dilly, testing them.

"No, but Jackson has heard it," said Clark.

Dilly looked at Jackson for confirmation.

"It's true, Mrs. Kilgour. Every year prior to Hallowe'en, I hear the whistle in the night and then I hear the bells clanging when it reaches the station."

"You can hear the bells all the way from Creekside?" she asked.

"No, I hear them when the train pulls into Black Springs Station."

Dilly looked steadily at the boys, holding back the memories and dread that welled within her at mention of the iron beast.

"The train seems to call directly to me but I don't know what to do," said Jackson. "We were hoping you'd come with us just once because you've had experience riding it."

Dilly wanted to shake them both. "If you have any sense at all, you will never attempt to ride that train," she said.

Nineteen

September was drawing to a close, the smell of autumn already in the air. In the meadow, Hilma was collecting herbs for Sister Helen while the theme of a fantasia she was learning for Sister Beatrice swirled through her head. Daisy and Shadow frolicked nearby, running, wrestling and crouching in spontaneous games of hide and seek.

Carefully Hilma combed the grasses for timothy, meadow fescue, sweet clover, trefoil, yarrow, chicory and sheep's parsley. She had always been impressed by her grandmother's knowledge of herbs but had never taken a personal interest. Since working with Sister Helen, she had become fascinated with the aromas and medicinal properties of plants.

Clover had tonic and blood-cleansing properties. Chicory contained minerals such as calcium, potassium, boron and zinc. Sheep's Parsley was mineral-rich, high in iron and vitamin C, good for kidney and bladder disease.

Some would find Hilma's variety of responsibilities confusing or draining but for Hilma, it was invigorating. She often marvelled at how many satisfying careers a person might pursue if one were granted an extended lifespan.

If I hadn't become a musician, I might have been a herbist or healer of some kind, she thought as she hummed and gathered. *I even enjoy my office responsibilities here most days.* Lost in thought, she did not hear the former caretaker's approach.

"What are you doing here, Miss Business Manager?" asked Claude, coming up behind her.

Startled, Hilma dropped her basket and whirled to face him.

"A better question is 'What are *you* doing here?'" she retorted, annoyed that her senses had not picked up his movement through the fields. "Aren't you supposed to be working for Dilly?"

"I'm taking a break," he said. "It's been a while since I've spent any time in the meadow and I just wanted to wander about for a few minutes for old times' sake."

Hilma bent to gather the scattered herbs and return them to the basket.

"Do you know the names of the grasses you're harvesting?" he asked.

"Most of them. Do you?"

"I know a few but the sisters didn't think I was smart enough to learn such things," he said. "As long as I was working from morning to night, they were happy."

"Was it really that bad?" she asked.

"I think the worst thing was not having a friend my age. Or maybe it was knowing that my own mother didn't want me."

He's probably had few opportunities to confide in anyone, thought Hilma.

"I was raised by my grandparents after my mother died," she said. "Is it not similar that you were raised by the sisters?"

"Did *you* feel lonely and neglected all the time?"

"I don't think so," she admitted.

"Well, I did," he said, anger and hurt registering in his eyes and the firm set of his jaw.

Hilma was trying to think of something reassuring to say when she heard a voice calling from the direction of the abbey. To Hilma's surprise, there was Sister Beatrice standing at the edge of the meadow, waving and shouting.

"I'll be right there," Hilma called back.

"Claude, I want to speak with you!" yelled the organist, ignoring Hilma.

Claude's jaw dropped and he looked genuinely frightened. "If you're heading back to the abbey now, could you walk with me?" he asked Hilma quietly.

Curious, Hilma picked up her basket of herbs and called to the dogs. Tails wagging and tongues lolling, they raced towards her. Claude trudged along woodenly. It struck Hilma that he seemed like a little boy afraid of Teacher.

"Take the herbs in to Sister Helen," said the organist to Hilma when they reached her. "I need a moment with Claude."

Not finding Sister Helen in the cloister garden, Hilma entered the abbey by the side door and climbed the stairs to the second floor. She found the herbist in her drying room and handed her the basket.

Then hearing voices emanating from the recreation room, she headed in that direction. Before she could stick her head through the door, she picked up a half-whispered conversation between her sister and Garth.

"I worry about her guarded behaviour," said Garth. "It's like she's always wearing armour."

"I think she's more guarded around you than with the rest of us, Garth," said Azur. "Perhaps she's grappling with her feelings for you."

"That's my hope," he sighed.

"Nonetheless, she seems to be gaining confidence since she's been working here," said Azur. "The responsibilities she's been given are definitely good for her."

"I didn't know her well before her … ordeal," said Garth. "Is she more like she was before then?"

Hilma heard silence while Azur mulled this over before answering. "I suppose I'd have to say that she still seems somewhat different than the sister I remember. Occasionally I do catch snatches of her former self. Hopefully, she just needs more time."

"Time." Garth repeated the word dully.

Hilma could restrain herself no longer. She entered the room, glaring angrily.

"Why does everyone have this burning desire to run my life?" she asked.

Garth and Azur stared at her like guilty children.

"Why can't you just accept that I'm…*different*, as you put it?"

"You're talking to other Sensos. Some would say we're all different when really, we're special."

"Do either of *you* see ghosts?" she demanded.

"What are you talking about?" asked Azur.

"Hilma saw a ghost in Providence Crossing flats," explained Garth. "It was the same day I drove her here to meet Aunt Jane."

"What did the ghost look like?" asked Azur.

"She had pale wavy hair and was dressed in a flowered skirt with a grey shawl wrapped around her shoulders."

"Are you sure it was a ghost? That description sounds rather detailed, not that I've ever seen a ghost."

"It was definitely a spirit of some kind. She was somewhat transparent and faded away."

"Have you seen her since?"

"No, but I've seen other ghosts in the abbey."

"You didn't tell me that," said Garth reproachfully.

"You didn't believe me about the first one."

"I did believe you about the ghost in the flats. I just couldn't see it," said Garth.

"Tell us about the other ghosts," said Azur.

Hilma sighed and took a seat.

"When Abbess took me up the back stairs after you left me at the abbey for lunch, I saw a girl with long brown hair on the third-floor landing. She was gone the next time I looked."

"That first day?" asked Garth.

"Yes."

"Why didn't you tell me?"

"Two ghosts in one day, neither of which you personally witnessed?"

"Did the girl say anything?" asked Azur.

"None of them have spoken," said Hilma.

Garth and Azur waited for her to continue.

"The next ghost I saw appeared the afternoon of the day I moved into the abbey. I was in the cloister garden with Sister Helen and she took me into the cemetery. A girl with short fair hair was standing near the Holy Family statue."

"Did Sister Helen see her?"

"No."

"Have there been others?" asked Garth.

"Oh, yes. The next one appeared in late July just before lunch. Actually, it was the day the twins were born. I saw a girl with short dark hair running through the meadow holding a baby. She looked at me when I called to her."

"And?" encouraged Azur.

"She faded away. What else would a ghost do?" asked Hilma, a tinge of self-deprecation in her voice.

"It's what one might expect," said Garth with a smile.

"I think Meri saw ghosts the day the Kilgours moved in," said Hilma.

"What makes you think so?" asked Azur.

"She wandered outside while Graeme and Dilly thought she was napping. Everyone in the abbey ran around looking for her until we found her outside picking wildflowers. She told us she'd been playing with the *big girls*."

Garth and Azur exchanged thoughtful looks.

"Okay, back to *my* ghosts. A few days after seeing the cemetery girl, I was in the chapel with Sister Beatrice when the girl with long brown hair dropped by to listen to me playing the organ."

"The same girl you saw on the third floor landing your first day here?" asked Azur.

"Yes, and without thinking, I told Sister Beatrice what I saw. It just slipped out."

"And her reaction?" asked Garth.

"It seemed to scare her, but surprisingly, she believed me. She told me the description could fit Myra, one of the penitents who loved music. I asked her about the other girls I'd seen, and Sister Beatrice wasn't sure about the fair-haired one. However, she felt the dark-haired one could have been Corinne, who took her newborn baby from the nursery and ran away. Myra went after them and the three were never seen again."

"Keep going," said Garth.

"Well, when Ethan was here in late August, he chased the fair-haired girl through the fields."

"Ethan saw her?" asked Azur.

"Actually he said he was chasing a white light, but I could see the girl."

"He never mentioned it to XT or me," said Azur. "But remember what he typed to you when he was leaving Mavis and Bram's with his parents?"

"He said there was danger at the abbey," said her sister.

"Do you know what he meant?" asked Garth.

"No."

"Do you feel you're in danger?"

"I find the spirit sightings disconcerting, but I haven't sensed danger. In fact, that's one of the things that bothers me. My sensointuitive acuity seems to have dulled."

"Why do you say that?"

"To give you a recent example, Claude came up behind me through the grasses and I didn't hear, smell or feel his presence."

"You were probably deep in thought," said Azur.

"You were likely relaxed for a change," said Garth. "It's normal and necessary to tune down perceptions from time to time."

"Keep in mind that being sensointuitive requires balancing sensory and intuitive intensity with everyday life," said Azur.

"I learned to maintain that balance while I was still a child," said Hilma.

"We all did," said Garth. "In your case, coping with anxiety since your return from Vapourlea has undoubtedly interfered with the balancing act."

"And seeing ghosts on top of that can't have helped," said Azur. "I'm annoyed that you didn't confide in us earlier."

Hilma smiled at the realization that, while they were meddling in her life as usual, this time she found it comforting.

"Why are you smiling?" asked Azur.

"It occurred to me that I like being with Sensos," said Hilma.

Garth and Azur eyed her suspiciously which made her laugh out loud.

"I have to get back to work," said Hilma, rising. "My desk is piled with invoices and memos."

"Since your duties include overseeing the renovations, I need your help in decorating my condo," said Garth.

"I'm not sure how good I'd be at masculine themes," said Hilma.

"I was hoping it would reflect your personal taste," said Garth.

Azur smiled and slipped from the room.

Twenty

Although Eula normally ate the evening meal with Hilma and the novices, it was unusual for her to join them for lunch as she did on the last day of September.

"I can't get into a writing mood at all today," she explained to them. "I must need a holiday."

"Will you be going somewhere?" asked Sister Jamini.

"I was just kidding," laughed the writer. "The abbey is my holiday. Where else would I be so spoiled and relaxed?"

"Do you ever get cabin fever?" asked Hilma.

"Not really," said Eula. "The sisters set a great example of living serenely and contentedly in a confined space."

"I don't feel like I'm in a confined space at all," said Sister Fazeela. "We're often outside in the cloister garden or beyond the walls mowing grass and cleaning up. And when we're inside, we have the entire abbey to move around in."

"Or we did until the renovations started," said her novice companion.

Hilma thought it interesting that the novices found it liberating to live within the borders of Black Springs Abbey. She wondered if Eula did. However, when she suggested that the writer accompany her outside while she exercised the dogs, Eula hesitated.

Then throwing aside her customary wariness, Eula agreed it might be fun. So immediately after lunch, she accompanied Hilma, Shadow and Daisy down the stairs, out the side door and into the meadow.

"It smells wonderful out here," she said, inhaling deeply. "The air is so fresh."

"You should come out more often," said Hilma.

"Perhaps next summer when they have trellises and gazebos out here," she conceded.

"It would be an ideal place to write," agreed Hilma."

"If I could be certain no one would intrude," said Eula.

"I'm sure even the children would learn to leave a working author undisturbed."

"I was thinking more of outside intruders."

"Are you really that afraid?"

"Unfortunately, I am."

Sensing that the writer wanted to confide in her, Hilma reached out and patted her arm encouragingly.

"Do you have time to listen to a story?" Eula asked her.

"I do."

Slowly, in bits and pieces, Eula described her marriage to Franklin Jennings, a wealthy widower with two teenage children. They met in a mall where she was signing books and he engaged her in conversation. She was young and naïve, he handsome and charming. In true fairytale fashion, he swept her off her feet and brought her to his mansion.

A couple of years into their marriage, she came to realize that his declining interest in coming to her bed was not due to aging. He was, it turned out, an unprincipled philanderer, maintaining a dutiful wife to manage his household and plan lavish dinner parties so that he could disappear for days on end to pursue business heavily mixed with pleasure.

Whenever she questioned him about rumors that had reached her ears, he flew into wild rages. She wanted to leave him but had no money of her own.

"What about your husband's wealth?" asked Hilma.

"As I said, I was very naïve," said Eula. "I had trustingly signed a prenuptial agreement before our wedding to reassure his children that I was not a gold digger. After all, I was confident that my loving husband would see to my every need. What a simpleton I was. His children hated me anyway."

"How did you handle expenses?"

"Franklin gave me a weekly allowance. In the early days of our marriage, I was awed by his generosity. He employed fashion experts to help me select an extensive wardrobe of clothing, shoes and handbags in the latest styles and colours. He regularly presented me with beautiful jewelry. Caterers looked after all the planning and serving at our many dinner parties. My duties were to select event themes, oversee that everything ran smoothly, and be gracious and welcoming."

"Did you find that stressful?" wondered Hilma.

"Initially I felt terrified and inadequate. But over time, it became routine."

"Didn't your books provide you with money?"

"My writing success is a recent development. After I decided to leave him, I didn't tell Franklin that I had begun writing mysteries under the pseudonym, Jay Pilgrim. Initially I arranged that my publisher hold my money in trust. When my books became unbelievably popular, I found a lawyer and financial advisor to handle everything including taxes. Both of them are still sworn to secrecy about my identity and whereabouts."

"It must have been a tremendous relief to have the freedom to take control of your life," said Hilma.

"Yes, to flee from my golden prison," said Eula.

"Still, I sense an inner sadness," said Hilma.

The writer sighed heavily as she strolled slowly along at Hilma's side. Finally she spoke. "I lost two children during the early years of my marriage. Our daughter was two years old and our son was four months old. They were both so beautiful."

"I'm truly sorry."

"Our daughter drowned in the pond behind our house and our son's death was attributed to sudden infant death syndrome. Both were in the care of nannies when it happened."

Hilma's whole being felt the writer's grief.

"A gardener found the bodies of our little girl and her nanny. It was thought the nanny had jumped in to save her and couldn't swim."

"How terrible," whispered Hilma.

"After our baby boy died, Franklin never touched me again. I think it was an excuse to stop pretending. I tried to contact the baby's nanny later only to learn she had died in a hit-run accident. I've never felt good about that."

"Because you found it suspicious that she was the second nanny to die?"

"Hers and the baby's. You see, when Franklin proudly showed the baby to his older son, Frankie had been rudely disinterested. It occurred to me, even at the time, that Frankie might see the baby as competition."

"Did Frankie live there?"

"Yes, he had his own suite, and still does."

"Is he single?"

"He's been in and out of relationships."

"Would he have an opportunity to harm the baby?" asked Hilma, fearing that she was beginning to sound like a detective.

"It's quite possible. I was out of the house attending a bridal shower for the daughter of one of Franklin's wealthy clients when the tragedy happened. I was mad with grief and kept under sedation for days. The funeral was a blur. Eventually, I took my suspicions to Franklin."

"How did your husband take it?" asked Hilma.

"He slapped my face and accused me of paranoia. It was the only time he struck me, but from that day on, I knew I would leave. Fortunately, I didn't know then that it would be nine years before I'd be able to execute my plan."

"Did your writing success make it possible?"

"It did, and I thank God every day," said Eula.

"Amen."

"Did you know that Abbess allowed me to hide my car in one of the abbey sheds in case anyone came nosing around?"

"Is it still here?"

"Yes, under lock and key. It's a black corvette stingray coupe. I'm afraid to have someone try to sell it for me in case the trail leads back to the abbey."

"Can't you get a restraining order?"

"A restraining order would be a joke to Franklin. You have no idea how devious he can be and what powerful connections he has through his corporation. But it's okay, Hilma. I'm content to live here as long as the nuns are willing to let me. Someday he'll die. His son and daughter will acquire all his wealth and they'll realize then that I'm not a threat to their inheritance."

"Does your family know where you are?"

"I have no family here. My parents are dead. I have a few cousins, whom I've never met, living in England."

"Isn't it difficult to live a life in hiding?"

"I'm still pondering what Abbess said to me when I first arrived at the abbey," said Eula.

"What did she say?"

"She said, 'It's important to recognize that from which one hides.'"

Hilma wondered why these words resonated in her own thoughts for the duration of her stroll with the writer and dogs.

Twenty-one

The Hallowmas *camp-in* at the home of Mavis and Bram Galvinston on Warren Avenue had become a tradition of sorts. In the five years since the Vapourlea rescue, Azur and XT had joined Hilma and the Galvinstons there during the week leading up to Hallowe'en. Hilma derisively called it "babysitting" but secretly found it comforting.

The Moonstorey sisters, Azur and Hilma, had been raised in this house by their grandparents and still called it home. With seven days remaining in October, they discussed the wisdom of staying in the abbey versus following their pre-Hallowe'en routine with Bram and Mavis.

"Have you by any chance heard the train whistle this October?" asked Azur, hoping for a reply in the negative.

"Unfortunately, that demon train has been calling me for three nights now," said Hilma with an involuntary shudder, dispelling her sister's hope.

Azur sighed. "Dilly and I both stopped hearing it when we were twenty-one and you've already passed that milestone."

"Guess I'm a late bloomer."

"XT and I are quite prepared to move to Warren Av tonight with you and the babies," said Azur.

"I think I'll be fine here," said Hilma.

"Are you sure?"

"I'm sure. I'm quite content to stay snuggled up in the abbey with all of you."

"Imagine you hearing that whistle so far away from Creekside."

"It sounded much closer than that," said Hilma. "More like it was approaching Black Springs than Creekside."

"I've never heard of timeriders boarding at Black Springs Station," said Azur.

"Nor I," said Hilma.

"Hope I'm not intruding, but I overheard that last snippet of conversation while I was passing by," said Dilly, setting down a basket of folded laundry. "Actually, Jackson told me that whenever he hears the Hallowmas train, it's approaching Black Springs, not Creekside."

"I take it Jackson is one of your co-op students and he just happens to be a Senso?"

"He claims to be," said Dilly. "He and Clark have been pestering me to accompany them on the train but I've discouraged them from entertaining that idea."

"Did you tell him you were too old to hear the train, never mind ride it?"

"I did, but just today they told me they'd be picking me up sometime after eleven thirty tonight. They were kidding, of course."

"Hilma was telling me she's been hearing the train whistle for three nights now," said Azur.

"What a shame. Surely this will be the last year, Hilma," sympathized Dilly. "You'll have peace like the rest of us oldsters once you outgrow the beast's power to send you signals."

"It can't happen soon enough," said Hilma.

"Interesting that you've been hearing it for three nights though," said Dilly.

"Why interesting?"

"For the past three nights Meri's been waking up crying and wanting me to sleep with her."

"Did she say what's wrong?" asked Hilma.

"We can only get out of her that it's a bad dream. She can't describe it. I wonder now if it's been the train."

"Hilma and I heard it the first October we moved in with Bram and Mavis," said Azur. "I was seven then and Hilma was five."

"I'm sure I heard it in my cradle," said Dilly. "Guess we'll have to be vigilant this time of year with our own children."

★ ★ ★

That night, with her parents asleep in the adjacent cell, Meri awaked and looked around cautiously. In the soft glow of her angel night light, she could see Gideon asleep in his nearby crib. And then she heard it, first the clack-clack-clack of an approaching train on tracks, then the whistle far away.

She would have called out to her mother as on previous occasions, but this night she realized that she had been wakened by a train and not by a strange bad dream. Meri loved trains and was thrilled whenever the family car had to stop at a crossing while a train sped noisily past. It was always disappointing when the flashing red lights stopped, the striped arm swung up and the train went clickety-clickety-clack off into the distance.

Meri heard the whistle again, and this time it seemed to be calling her. She listened and was sure she heard her name carried on the wind. *Meri, Meri.* She giggled, picked up her blanket and walked barefoot into the dimly lighted corridor.

When she reached the end of the hall, Daisy rose from her dog bed to greet the child through the privacy gate separating the nuns' quarters from that of the new residents. The dog looked at her quizzically and wagged its tail. Meri reached through the gate to pet the soft furry muzzle.

"Shh," she whispered. "We have to be quiet."

The child went through the back exit and shut the door gently behind her. Daisy whined and returned to her bed.

Holding the railing tightly, Meri descended the stairs. The door to the outside was locked so she tugged on the bolt until it slipped free.

"Hi, Meri," said a friendly voice as soon as she stepped out into the cold night.

The child looked up in surprise to see Jackson and Clark standing there with three other teenagers, two girls and a boy.

"What are you doing here?" she asked them. "It's too dark to paint the barn."

"We were hoping to meet your mother," said Jackson. "We told her we'd be picking her up."

"Mommy doesn't come out in the dark," said the child.

"So why are *you* out here?" asked one of the girls, bending to touch the child's face.

"The train called me," said Meri. "Did it call you too?"

"It called all of us except Clark," said Jackson.

"We better get going, guys," said Clark, annoyed that the topic of his shortcomings had entered the conversation.

"Look at the sky! It's all glittery with stars. And the moon is like a cradle," said Meri looking up in wonder at the night sky.

"It's beautiful," said the girls in unison, staring at the spectacle that had captivated Meri.

"No time for star gazing," said Clark. "It's almost midnight and we have to meet your train."

"Come on, sweetie," said one of the girls, taking Meri's hand and pulling her towards the car.

"I'm not dressed and I don't have shoes," protested Meri.

"You'll be fine," said the girl. "You've got your blanket."

"Where are we going?" asked Meri trying to pull away.

"To see the train that's been calling us," said Jackson. "Your Mommy will follow us as soon as she finds you missing. Then we can all ride the train together."

"Okay," said Meri, dubiously, allowing herself to be assisted onto the lap of one of the three teenagers who had squeezed into the car's back seat.

Jackson deliberately slammed his car door loudly and beeped the horn three times before driving away in a noisy scrunch of tires on gravel.

"That should get Mrs. Kilgour's attention," he said with satisfaction.

Twenty-two

Graeme, XT, and Garth stepped into the corridor in response to the noise made by the departing car and the insistent barking of the dogs. Daisy was now whimpering at the gate while Shadow growled and paced.

"Someone left in a hurry," said Graeme.

"If it was a medical emergency, the nuns would have called for me or Azur," said XT, puzzled.

"Meri's not in her bed!" said Dilly, bursting from her children's room.

Shadow whined and took a few steps toward the exit, his body language indicating that he wished to be followed.

"I'm going outside with Shadow," said Garth, who had slipped into shoes and was now throwing on a jacket over his pajamas.

As he neared the exit, Hilma came up to the privacy gate wearing slippers and a robe.

"What's going on?" she asked him.

"Meri's missing."

"Oh, no! She must have heard the train whistle!" cried Hilma, flinging open the gate.

"Why do you say that?" asked Garth.

"Because it called me too. We have no time to lose!"

By this time, Azur and Dilly had joined them, wearing hastily donned jackets and shoes. Dilly was frantic.

"I'll stay with the children," volunteered XT, earning a grateful nod from Graeme who then raced down the stairs and exited the building with the others. There was no sign of Meri near the abbey.

"The car sounds we heard must have been the boys coming for me," said Dilly. "Instead they took Meri."

"What car sounds?" asked Hilma. "From my side, I only heard the dogs barking."

"What boys?" Graeme asked his wife.

"The co-op students. They wanted me to board the train with them."

Graeme looked at her in shock. "You knew they were coming?"

"Of course not!" she snapped, angry that he should think her so irresponsible.

"We've got to hurry!" said Hilma urgently. "The whistle has stopped and now I hear the bells! The train's at the station!"

"I'll drive," said Azur, running for her car, the others at her heels.

Five humans and one canine clambered into the car and sped off into the night.

"Where are we going?" asked Azur.

"Black Springs Station," said Dilly.

"The building's been moved to the Canadian Oil Museum," said Graeme.

"Would the train go there or to its original location in town?" wondered Garth.

"I don't know," said Dilly, her voice rising anxiously. "What do you think, Hilma?"

"No idea," said Hilma in dismay.

"Head for the museum first," Garth instructed Azur. "It's on our way."

"Hilma, since you're the only one of us who can hear the train, you'll probably be the only one to see it," said Azur to her sister who sat tensely beside her in the front. "If Meri's already on board, you'll have to go in after her alone."

"Don't worry. I can do that," said Hilma, her heart hammering wildly.

"I can't believe those boys would take little Meri to lure me to the train," moaned Dilly, holding her head in anguish.

Graeme fumed in silence, contemplating what he would do to the boys when he got his hands on them.

"It's a good sign that those kids deliberately created a commotion so they'd be followed," said Garth reassuringly to the distraught parents.

"Should the train depart before you and Meri can get off, you must remain on board the train when it reaches Prosper Station," Azur told her sister. "And don't let any of the others get off either."

"I won't."

"Keep everyone on board until the return trip to Black Springs," said Dilly.

"I will."

"Will you be able to resist Vek?" asked Garth anxiously.

"I'll have to," said Hilma.

"You need to memorize Zhiab's mantra in order to fend off the Faefumes who might meet the train at Prosper Station," said Azur.

"Teach me," said Hilma, fearfully recalling her misadventure five years ago.

"The darkness is never darkness to the One," said Dilly from the back seat.

"The darkness is never darkness to the One," repeated Hilma.

"Mavis said it's from a Psalm," said Azur. "'Even the darkness is not dark for you; the night is as bright as the day, for darkness is as light to you.'"

"So what is Zhiab's mantra again?" asked Hilma nervously.

Azur and Dilly answered in unison and everyone in the car joined in, reciting the mantra over and over. It seemed to bolster their confidence as they made their way down the back roads leading to Gum Bed Line. As they raced toward the site of the oil museum, the smell of oil from the Fairbank oilfield seemed especially pungent that October night.

To their dismay, when they reached the museum, they found the entrance barred by an iron pipe gate. Beyond the barrier, a pair of yard lights cast an eerie glow over the site. In the distance, the museum and its outbuildings were in darkness.

Leaving the vehicle parked outside the gate, they ran towards the restored train station, feet pelting over lawn and boardwalk. Garth shone his flashlight through the windows into the dark interior of the waiting room, its pale walls contrasting against the dark wood of floor, wainscoting and benches.

Hilma peered over his shoulder as the beam of light glanced around the unoccupied room and traced across the round middle of the cast iron potbelly stove.

"Back to the original depot site!" she yelled.

Accompanied by Shadow, the five tore across the yard and through the entrance gate. Panting from exertion and fear, they scrambled into the waiting car.

"Where are we going?" asked Azur, turning the key in the ignition and backing the car out onto the road.

"Black Springs," said Hilma.

"Turn left on Kelly Road and left again on Victoria," directed Garth.

The occupants of Azur's car scarcely noticed where the glow of street lights marked their arrival to the sleeping village. They were similarly oblivious to jack-o-lanterns, skeletons, witches and ghosts, Hallowe'en props for the handful of darkened houses on Victoria Street.

"Stop here," said Garth after a right turn on Margaret Street. "This is where the train depot was."

"On a parking lot across from a laundromat and carwash?" asked Azur, bringing her vehicle to an abrupt halt.

The parking lot was dark and empty except for a single unoccupied car.

"There's nothing here," cried Dilly.

"God help us," said Graeme.

"I see it!" shouted Hilma.

She leapt from Azur's car, ran onto the empty parking lot and faded from their sight.

Hastily exiting the vehicle, her companions followed and stood about helplessly. Shadow sniffed the ground and whined.

★ ★ ★

Bells clanging, the black iron monster waited impatiently to depart as Hilma stumbled towards it on slippered feet. She raced across the tracks to reach the boarding side and jumped in fright when it sent a hissing blast of steam her way. She looked up to see the numbers 330 emblazoned on its face. Steam Engine 330, the same engine that had previously delivered her to what had become a year-long nightmare.

The only figure on the wooden boarding platform between train and depot was Clark looking dejected and miserable.

"Are they on board?" Hilma asked him.

"I guess so," said Clark. "The others managed to get me this far, but then they disappeared."

"Is Meri with them?"

"Yeah," he mumbled.

Grabbing the rail, Hilma climbed the steps connecting the platform to the iron hulk towering above. Before she could reach the coach doorway, a uniformed man stepped out and blocked her way. He was smartly attired in navy blue, his vest and jacket adorned with polished brass buttons, his black pill box with grey braid and a brass plate.

Hilma did not need to read the word etched thereon. She knew it bore the title, *CONDUCTOR*, because it was the same conductor who had accompanied her on her previous journey.

"Your ticket, Mademoiselle," he said, holding out his white-gloved hand.

"I don't have one."

"There might still be time to get one in the depot," he said calmly.

"You'll wait for me?" she asked.

"It will depend on the train's schedule."

In the soft glow of the gas lamps dimly illuminating the depot, Hilma could make out wooden benches dispersed around a central waiting room and the potbelly stove she had seen through the station window at the museum. She rushed up to the ticket office and was handed a double ticket.

"Remember to tuck away your return portion," advised the agent. "That is, if you plan to return." He chuckled at his own humour.

Same ticket agent as in Providence Crossing five years ago and same sick humour, thought Hilma bitterly.

"Your luggage, Miss?" asked a baggage handler, appearing out of nowhere.

"I don't have any," said Hilma, tightening the belt of her robe

"You may want to change into something more appropriate on arrival," he said, eying her suggestively.

Hilma raced back to the train, clutching her ticket. The conductor was awaiting her on the platform.

"You'll find the little red-headed lass inside," he said. "Looks just like your sister's friend. Bet it's her daughter."

Hilma said nothing.

"Are you surprised I remember?" he asked.

"Remember what?"

"You and your sister and her friend. I also remember the lanky fellow with the crazy cat."

Hilma almost laughed at the man's description of XT and Bleu, the Galvinston cat. Almost, but didn't. The present grim situation in which she found herself quickly stifled any mirth.

"Can I board now?" she asked.

Watch your step," he said, taking her by the elbow to assist her onto the bottom step.

Entering the vintage coach, Hilma was relieved to see Meri sitting in the second rows of leather seats which, as before, were elegantly draped in lace backcloths. A teenage girl sat with the child and a second girl sat in the row behind them. Jackson was in the front with another youth.

"Where's Mommy?" asked the child, leaving her place to run to Hilma.

"Come sit with me," said Hilma, taking the little hand and leading her to the empty fourth row.

She guided the child into the window seat and sank breathlessly beside her.

"Where's Mommy?" repeated Meri.

"Your mommy sent me instead, but you'll see her soon," said Hilma.

"I want to see her now," said Meri, tears welling in her eyes.

"Yes, where is Mrs. Kilgour?" demanded Jackson, walking down the aisle to confront Hilma. "Doesn't she care about her daughter?"

"Get back to your seat!" ordered Hilma. "You've put all our lives in jeopardy."

Before Jackson could respond, the train lurched forward, pushing him off balance. He returned to his seat and, through the window, saw his friend, Clark, standing forlornly on the platform.

Twenty-three

Announcing its departure in hissing steam and clanging bells, the iron beast rumbled away from Black Springs Station.

"Sit back and enjoy the ride," said the conductor as the train picked up speed.

Peering through glass windows into the outer blackness, the timeriders could see only their reflections until they entered a tunnel. Then they could make out rough stone walls flashing past, illuminated dimly in the light of the coach's oil lamps. The walls soon blurred into fluidic streaks when the iron beast seemed to leave the tracks.

Pushed back into their seats by the gravitational force of the beast's flight, they grasped the carriage arms until they could again feel tracks beneath the speeding coach.

"Your tickets, Ladies and Gentlemen," said the conductor pleasantly.

He returned the punched tickets to the riders who gaily stowed them away. Meri prudently handed hers to Hilma who deposited it, along with her own, in her robe pocket.

As soon as the conductor exited the carriage, Hilma stood up and addressed the young adventurers.

"Listen to me carefully," she told them firmly. "When the conductor returns with refreshments, you must eat slowly because I have very important things to tell you before you go to sleep."

"I don't intend to go to sleep," said the girl who had been sitting with Meri.

"Please pay attention," said Hilma. "You will all be sleeping whether you want to or not."

She went on to tell them that the most important thing for them to remember was that they absolutely must stay on board when the train arrived at Prosper Station. To disembark would mean no possibility of return until All Souls Day.

"That's more than a week from now, and in that time, you could be imprisoned forever," she warned.

Five pair of eyes looked at her gravely.

"We thought it was all a lark," said the boy sitting with Jackson.

"Believe me, it is no lark," said Hilma. "Most timeriders who board this train never see their families again."

"You did," said Jackson.

"Only because I was rescued by some very courageous people who risked their lives for me."

"I want to go home," cried Meri, tears coursing down her face.

"Don't worry, honey, you will be going home because you and I will not leave the train until it returns to Black Springs. Whether or not our high school friends go with us will be up to them."

Hilma gave her audience a quick history of early Black Springs, home of the first commercial oil business in North America. As early as the 1860s, a thousand wells produced twelve thousand barrels of oil daily and the population swelled to 4000 people. She told them how because of the technology available in those early days, there were frequent fires, nitroglycerine explosions and gas vapours everywhere. She shared with them a summary of the knowledge passed on to her by her grandmother, that toxicity in the environment caused genetic mutations in some of the region's population.

"Our sensointuitive gene is a mutation?" asked one of the teens.

"I thought it was a gift," said another.

Hilma impressed upon them that, being gifted with acute sensory aptitudes and intuitive skills, Sensointuitives had a corresponding duty to use their abilities wisely and generously.

She explained to them that when they arrived in Prosper Station, they would meet other mutants. A few would be sensointuitive humans like themselves, but they'd also encounter shape shifters called Novapetrols and Faefumes.

"Novapetrols will assist you," she said. "They provide protection to time travellers and seem to sense when a timerider is in danger. You'll recognize Novapetrols by their blue colouration."

"Excuse me, Miss Moonstorey. You keep mentioning Prosper Station," said Jackson.

"Prosper Station is the Victorian dimension of modern Creekside. More frighteningly, it's the access venue to Vapourlea. This train will stop there, but I repeat, you must not get off!"

Hilma told the young timeriders about the green psychic vampires called Faefumes who emitted seductive fumes while absorbing their victims' vitality and energy. She emphasized that they were evil, dangerous and devious.

"They will go to any length to lure you off this train," she said.

"But you won't let go of me, will you, Hilma," said Meri. It was not a question, but a statement begging reassurance.

"I will never, *ever* let you go," said Hilma.

"Your tea, Ladies and Gentlemen," said the conductor, entering their coach with a linen-covered cart. With practiced gentility, he set portable tables before each passenger, covered each table with a linen cloth and placed serviettes upon each timerider's lap. Then he distributed pots of fragrant tea and passed around plates of fancy sandwiches and mini-cakes. Bowing, he left them to enjoy their refreshments.

"Before you touch a single bite, you must memorize the mantra taught me by the guardian, Zhiab," Hilma insisted.

Convinced by this time of the seriousness of their situation, the teenagers left their food untouched and recited the mantra over and over until Hilma was satisfied.

"The darkness is never darkness to the One… The darkness is never darkness to the One…The darkness is never darkness to the One… The darkness …"

Given a nod of permission from Hilma, they turned to the refreshments set invitingly before them. They exchanged smiles with each other as they sipped tea from a gold-rimmed china cups bearing the railway logo. They eagerly reached for the dainty sandwiches arranged on matching china plates.

When Hilma returned to sit beside Meri, the child smiled up at her in relief. After the first few bites, Hilma felt unaccountably famished. She noticed that Meri also was happily eating away.

Soon every mouthful of tea and crumb of sandwich and cake was gone. Silently, the conductor returned to remove the dishes and tables.

Then lulled by clacking rails and gently swaying cars, the passengers borne into the night by Steam Engine 330 nodded off.

"Prosper Station!" called the conductor.

The timeriders awoke to the sounds of engine brakes and clanging bells announcing their arrival. The brutish machine gave some final snorts and hisses before coming to a convulsive stop.

Rising from their seats to better see what lay outside their windows, the passengers observed a wooden walkway dimly lit by a single gas lamp. Running in a north-south direction along the tracks, the walkway was perpendicular to a raised platform reached by six wide steps.

The depot was an unpretentious two-storied wooden structure, its lower windows illuminated by flickering oil lamps, the upper windows black.

"Sit down and remain in your seats," said Hilma sternly.

The young timeriders obeyed.

"All out for Prosper Station," said the conductor, standing expectantly at the coach door.

"We forgot our luggage," said Jackson.

The other teenagers tittered in appreciation of his wit.

"Time to get out, young ladies and gents," said the conductor. "You'll find accommodations nearby."

"We forgot our money," said one of the girls to more laughter.

"Timeriders are welcomed free of charge in Prosper Station," said the conductor amiably. "So are you ready to get off, young timeriders?"

"Let's just take a quick look around town," suggested one of the teen girls.

"We'll never have another chance to see a real Victorian town," said the other girl.

"But it's the middle of the night. What would we see?" asked the boy sitting beside Jackson.

"Ladies of the night and bar brawls," said Hilma.

The teens laughed.

"I wasn't being funny," said Hilma. "You're not leaving the train."

The teenage timeriders groaned.

Hilma looked out her window and noticed green glowing forms approaching through the darkness from all directions.

"Look out the window!" she gasped.

They peered into the night and at first saw nothing alarming. Then one of the girls screamed.

"What?" asked Jackson.

"Green things! Coming towards us!" cried the girl.

"Are they Faefumes, Hilma?"

"Say the mantra with me," she urged. "Now!"

Terrified, they needed no further prompting. Meri closed her eyes tightly and joined the teenagers as they chanted. "The darkness is never darkness to the One… The darkness is never darkness to the One…"

Twenty-four

Attended by several Faefumes, Vek sauntered over to the train and stood beneath Hilma's window. Shape shifter that he was, he stretched his body until his gaze was level with hers as she sat trembling beside Meri.

"Hilma, my favourite, you've returned," he said, his voice as clear as if no glass separated them. "And you're accompanied by an adorable little timerider with beautiful red curls."

Mesmerized by his glittering round eyes, Hilma was unable to avert her gaze.

"I'm scared," said Meri.

The child's voice triggered a protective instinct within her.

"Say the mantra," she said, and the child began to chant.

Freed from Vek's hypnotic gaze by the child's intonation, Hilma turned to the others. "Say the mantra," she ordered them. But overwhelmed by the sight of the gathering Faefume horde, the teenagers had become mute.

Sensing his advantage, Vek sidled over to the teenage girls' window. Eyes fixed straight ahead, they clung to each other.

"Welcome, welcome, dear ladies," said the Faefume. "Come with me and you can be princesses in my wonderful domain."

The girls whimpered and trembled.

Vek then peered in at Jackson and his friend. "My dear young gentlemen, join me and become knights in shiny armour in my enchanted kingdom."

"Timeriders!" shouted Hilma. "He's evil, a liar! Recite the mantra. Save yourselves!"

By this time, several Faefumes had crowded up the train steps and stood in the carriage doorway blowing their noxious fumes into the air within. Intoxicated by the vapours, the teenagers were unable to focus on anything but the hopelessness of the situation in which they found themselves. The words of the recitation Hilma had taught them stuck in their throats.

Then they became aware of a new presence among them. A handsome mutant with dark almond-shaped eyes, long black hair and blue skin stood in the aisle, penetrating their consciousness with a compelling serenity.

"Timeriders," he said, "you must listen to Hilma. Recite the mantra which will guard you from the evil surrounding you."

"Zhiab, thank heavens you're here," whispered Hilma, tears of relief filling her eyes.

"Hilma," said the guardian, "you have the responsibility of protecting these young people. Turn on your sensory powers. Pray the mantra."

As Hilma waited for further words of encouragement, the Novapetrol guardian faded away.

"No! Don't leave us!" cried Hilma. "Zhiab? Where are you?"

The Faefumes laughed, breathing poisonous gases into the carriage with each exhalation, savouring the scent of humans when they inhaled. The teenagers sat numbly in their seats, eyes glazing over. Only Meri remained alert, haltingly reciting the mantra between sobs.

Hilma was also succumbing to the fumes. She shook her head to clear the fog that threatened to overtake her. *Responsibility of protecting these young people... turn on sensory powers... pray the mantra.* Zhiab's words of counsel filled her mind.

The train was now surrounded by green forms reaching out with wavy, snake-like arms.

"Come with us. Come with us," they chanted in sing-song voices.

"No!" screamed Hilma angrily. "We are going home!"

Dizzy from fumes, she rose from her seat and staggered to the front of the coach, accompanied by Meri who clung tightly to her hand. Behind her back, the Faefumes laughed and leered.

"The darkness is never darkness to the One… The darkness is never darkness to the One…," she said, struggling to keep upright. "The darkness is never darkness to the One… The darkness …"

Through blurry vision, she saw the teenagers propped limply like mannequins in the leather seats, heads lolling against the lace backcloths. In her mind, the luxury of the carriage melded into a vision of the gloom and entrapment of Vapourlea.

Still reciting the mantra, she forced herself to move from row to row, shaking the dazed timeriders with as much strength as she could muster. She called upon divine power and willed herself to focus on her own inner strength.

"The darkness is never darkness to the One… The darkness is never darkness to the One…," she said urgently to each one.

Soon the young timeriders began to mumble the words, "The darkness is never darkness to the One…" After a few repetitions of the chant, their voices gained strength and clarity. They opened their eyes and sat erect.

Bewildered, the Faefumes found that they could no longer send fumes into the carriage. It was as if an invisible barrier had been erected between them and their human prey.

Outside the train, Vek's voice pleaded. "If you don't want to go to Vapourlea, at least spend Hallowmas in the delightful town of Prosper Station for the experience of a lifetime."

"Don't be deceived," said Hilma to her youthful companions. "If you leave this train, he will never let you go. You will never again see your families and friends. Stay where you are and keep chanting."

Acknowledging her leadership, the timeriders kept chanting, "The darkness is never darkness to the One…"

Programmed to its timetable, the train engine groaned and belched out steam. The bells began to urgently clang.

"Last chance for departure at Prosper Station," called out the conductor.

Hilma continued to lead her fellow passengers in a determined chant. "The darkness is never darkness to the One... The darkness is never darkness to the One..."

"Return to me, Hilma," called Vek. "Bring the little girl with you and come back to Vapourlea."

"Come back to Vapourlea, come back to Vapourlea," sang the horde of green figures in quavery voices.

The conductor hesitated before pulling up the steps. "Sorry, my friends," he said to the Faefumes as he closed the coach door.

Howls and shrieks from the outraged horde rose in the night air.

At that moment, the train lurched forward, and the timeriders exchanged cautiously hopeful glances as it rolled away from Prosper Station. Once outside town, the iron beast gave a wailing farewell whistle as it picked up speed.

Engine vibrations and the clack of train wheels upon steel rails blended into a rhythmic refrain. Peering into the outer darkness, the passengers saw their faces reflecting back at them in the polished glass. As on the previous trip, the train soon entered a tunnel carved into rock. It went ever faster until the stone walls blurred and the train seemed to leave the tracks. Pushed back into their seats, the passengers instinctively grasped the leather coach arms until they could again feel tracks beneath them.

"Tickets, please," said the conductor, standing in the aisle.

The riders searched through their pockets and pouches and handed them over.

"I'll be right back with refreshments," said the conductor.

"Guess I can say good-bye to my co-op placement," said Jackson morosely.

"Indeed," said Hilma flatly.

"Guess I'm in big trouble," he said.

"That goes without saying."

The conductor pushed the serving cart into the carriage aisle and set out linens, tea and tasty delicacies on the logo-ed china as before. The timeriders ate silently, reflecting on their near escape. When they finished eating and drinking, the conductor wheeled the empty dishes to the back of the car, and the passengers nodded off to sleep."

"Black Springs!" announced the conductor.

The passengers stirred themselves awake as Steam Engine 330 braked to a stop, announcing its arrival in surly snorts, angry hisses and clanging bells.

Assisted from the coach by the conductor, the timeriders descended the iron stairs. They sighed in relief until they noticed that they were on a wooden boarding platform dimly lit by a single gas lamp. The dark outline of the wooden station was eerily visible nearby.

"We haven't returned home!" gasped one of the teens.

The timeriders looked about in shock and horror.

Meri began to cry.

Then, in a flash, the scene changed. The train and conductor disappeared as did the gas lamp, the boarding platform and the wooden station.

The timeriders were on the Margaret Street parking lot in Black Springs. A train whistle sounded from afar, wailing forlornly in concert with the howling wind.

Waiting anxiously in the darkened parking lot, Azur, Dilly, Graeme and Garth saw Hilma walking towards them holding Meri's hand. They ran towards them, crying and laughing, and enveloped them in lingering hugs and exclamations of relief. Shadow wagged his tail in exuberant greeting.

"I didn't like that scary train," said Meri. "There were ugly green things that tried to steal me."

"I know, baby," said Dilly, holding her daughter close. "But now you're safe with Mommy and Daddy."

After he had hugged and kissed his daughter, Graeme turned his attention to Jackson and his teenage companions who huddled anxiously nearby.

"I hope this experience is indelibly impressed upon your brains," he said flatly.

"Yes, Sir," they replied contritely.

"I'll be meeting with you and your parents later today."

Nervously, they glanced at one another.

While Graeme was talking to the students, Garth came to stand beside him. The teens eyed the constable warily.

"You do realize you could be charged with kidnapping, amongst other things," he said. "I intend to be present when Mr. Kilgour talks to your parents."

The teens stood in fearful silence.

"Get in your car and go home," said Garth. "Now!"

"Yes, Sir," they mumbled, hurrying towards Jackson's parked vehicle.

Twenty-five

Hilma was exhausted the following day, but she managed to drag herself from bed and put in a morning's office work. After lunch, she told the sisters that she was going to retire to her room for the remainder of the day.

"Are you not feeling well?" asked the abbess.

Rather than explain the adventure she had endured during the night, Hilma merely nodded. "I'll be fine after a few hours rest," she said.

"I suppose that means you won't be coming for your organ lesson this afternoon," said Sister Beatrice.

"Sorry," said Hilma.

"Are we working you too hard?" asked Sister Helen.

Hilma smiled at the porter and assured her that, if anything, the abbey nuns were spoiling her.

"Did you hear the dogs barking in the night?" asked the organist.

"I did, but they seemed to settle down after a while," said Hilma evasively.

"It's unusual for them to act that way," said Sister Colleen. "There must have been racoons or some other wildlife rooting around outside."

"It was more than dogs that disturbed our sleep," said the organist. "I heard people running around on the north corridor."

"Garth told me they were up investigating the dog barking," explained the abbess.

"Are dogs really a good idea here?"

"We've always had a dog, Beatrice, and I don't recall you ever contributing to its care," said Sister Helen.

The organist sniffed.

Hilma excused herself and went to her room. Her head had barely touched the pillow when she fell soundly asleep. She did not awaken until Eula knocked softly on her door and asked her if she was going to supper.

"I'm not hungry," Hilma told the writer. "I'll get myself something from the kitchenette later."

Awake now, she padded to the washroom, took a drink of water and returned to bed to indulge in some reading. Propped up on pillows, she was contentedly reading until her senses told her she was not alone. She looked up from her book to find one of the three spirit girls, the one with short blond hair, standing by her bed.

The girl watched Hilma somberly before moving to stand by the door.

"It's hard to concentrate with a ghost in one's room, even though you're not as threatening as a Faefume," Hilma said.

Silently inviting Hilma to follow, the girl disappeared through the door. Curious, Hilma looked into the hallway and saw the girl waiting at the end of the hall near the nuns' quarters.

"Okay, I'm coming," she muttered.

She followed the girl into the west hall and through the privacy gate. From here, she could hear the clinking of dishes, snatches of conversation and spontaneous laughter as the residents enjoyed supper.

The girl was now at the stairs door. Hilma shrugged and followed her down to the side entrance.

"I'm glad it's still daylight because, after last night, I won't be going out in the dark," she said, opening the door.

"Hello, Hilma," said Claude, causing Hilma to jump from the unexpectedness of his appearance.

"Hello," she replied cautiously.

"Who were you talking to as you opened the door?" he asked.

"No one," said Hilma, realizing he had overheard her comment to the spirit girl.

"I sometimes talk to myself too," he said with a chuckle.

"Are you looking for someone?" she asked.

"Not really. I just finished work and thought I'd slip over to see how the renovations are coming along. I saw the workmen leave and I figured everybody else would be at supper."

"I'm sure the abbess will take you on a tour sometime."

"Do you think I could take a peek now?" he asked.

"I suppose I could show you some of the main floor level," said Hilma, seeing that the spirit girl had disappeared.

"Oh, thank you," said the man.

"If you come through this door, you'll be able to see how they've divided up the kitchen and laundry rooms into smaller, more suitable areas."

Claude followed Hilma into the old kitchen and looked about admiringly.

"This will be very nice for the sisters," he said.

"What are you doing here?" asked a sharp voice, startling them both.

They turned to see Sister Beatrice glaring at them.

"I was on my way home from finishing up some work for Dilly," stammered the former groundskeeper.

"She's Mrs. Kilgour to you, Claude. Or she should be." The nun paused to let her words sink in. "And are you on a first name basis with Miss Moonstorey as well?"

"No, Sister," he mumbled.

"You haven't explained yet how you got inside," said the organist.

Claude shuffled his feet.

"I let him in to have a look around," said Hilma, coming to the man's defense.

"Well the tour is over," declared the nun.

With a farewell bob of his head, Claude almost ran from the site.

As soon the door shut behind him, Sister Beatrice turned on Hilma. "Too tired for your afternoon duties but you can meet secretly with Claude," she said tartly.

"Why would I be meeting secretly with an old man?" retorted Hilma.

"I have no idea, especially when you're so taken with the constable."

Although she was incredulous at the organist's audacity, Hilma held her tongue.

"It's a good thing I was on my way to the chapel to prepare some liturgy for All Saints Day," said Sister Beatrice.

"Why was it a good thing?"

"A proper young lady would not place herself in an unseemly position."

"It's hurtful that you would make insinuations without evidence," said Hilma.

"Perhaps you can explain then," said the nun.

Hilma took a deep breath. "If you must know, I was following a spirit out to the meadow, and when I opened the door, Claude happened to be standing there."

Sister Beatrice blinked her eyes.

"It was the blonde girl I first saw in the cemetery," said Hilma.

"Such nonsense," sputtered the nun.

"You believed me about the girl in the chapel. What was her name? Myra?"

"I've thought that over since then, and I no longer find it plausible. You must have seen a shadow or a flicker of light from the stain glass windows."

"If you didn't find it believable, why did you tell me not to say anything to Abbess?"

"I didn't want Mother Abbess to think less of you for fabricating tales about a haunted abbey."

Hilma seriously doubted this.

"Well, I'm going to tell her now," she said. "I can't keep this to myself anymore."

"The abbess will sneer at such drivel."

"Then I'll have Garth accompany me when I tell her."

"Surely Garth doesn't believe in ghosts."

"He believes me and I think you do too."

The organist seemed to consider her response. Finally, she spoke. "When we were in the chapel, you caught me off guard with your realistic description of two girls who once lived in the abbey. I should never have given you names."

"But you did, and now I want you to name the girl with short fair hair."

"There were several blond girls. I couldn't possibly remember."

Suddenly the spirit girl reappeared. She tilted her head to one side, exposing a birthmark on her neck. Then she faded away.

"Would it help your memory if I told you the girl had a heart-shaped birthmark on her neck?"

The nun's mouth hung open for several long seconds.

"You know who she is, don't you?" persisted Hilma.

"I have work to do and it's getting late," said the organist, turning to walk quickly in the direction of the chapel.

Twenty-six

On the morning of All Hallows Eve, Garth invited Hilma to accompany him to the condominium he hoped would be *their* home. They walked through rooms smelling of fresh paint, admiring the tranquil effect created by the colours they had chosen together, off white with accent walls in blue and green.

"Throw cushions on the windows seats will add a cosy touch," said Hilma, standing near one of the gable windows.

"Will you come with me on my next day off to pick out furniture?" he asked.

"What about your furniture in storage?"

"It's not suitable for here."

Hilma looked around the spacious living room with what she hoped was a decorator's eye. "Furnishing this room will take some thought," she said.

"Especially with your harp and cello as the centre pieces," said Garth, wrapping his arm around her waist and pulling her close.

Hilma leaned against him briefly, but when she moved away and turned to look at him, he was troubled by the conflict reflected in her eyes. He fingered the small velvet box in his pocket and hesitated. To buy time, he suggested they take the dogs for a walk.

Out in the meadow, they walked silently hand in hand, comfortable in each other's company, yet unsettled by Hilma's unspoken doubts.

"Hilma, you do know how much I love you," he finally said.

"I love you too."

Then, sensing that he was about to seek more commitment from her than she was capable of giving, she sighed deeply and shared her troubled thoughts. Choosing her words cautiously, she told him how she lived in fear of appearing incompetent and of disappointing everyone she cared about yet again. She tried to explain how she perceived people being wary and careful around her, as if she might break. Since he hadn't yet asked the anticipated question, she stopped short of saying that she most likely lacked wifely qualities, whatever these might be.

Garth stopped walking and gently wiped away her tears.

"You're so hard on yourself, sweetheart," he said. "People are not being *wary and careful* around you, as you put it. They're listening to your opinions, treating you with *respect*, the respect due a business manager who's doing an exemplary job. Not only that, but they're impressed, as I am, with how well you handle organ lessons with the dragon lady. It seems to me that you've been handling stress exceptionally well."

Hilma sighed again, this time in relief. She even laughed at his reference to the formidable Sister Beatrice.

"I haven't even touched upon your incredible selflessness and bravery in boarding the Hallowmas train with Meri and those bratty kids," he continued. "I was terrified I'd never see you again.

"But I was the only one of you who could do that," she protested. "I had no choice."

"That's what courage is, finding yourself in a position to help and acting on it without regard to your own safety."

"Aren't you concerned about my ghost stories?"

"We can get to the bottom of the ghost thing together."

"Do you believe me then…about the spirit girls?"

"Yes, because I know how sincere and trustworthy you are."

He pulled her close and, surrounded by the whispering grasses of autumn, they clung to each other and kissed.

"I want to spend forever with you," he murmured into her hair. "Will you marry me?"

"Yes," she whispered, scarcely believing how magical that single world-altering word of consent could be.

Hilma could barely see through her tears as Garth reached into his pocket and opened a red velvet box containing a gold band encircled with tiny ruby and opal stones.

"Our birthstones," she said softly when he placed the ring on her finger. "It's the most beautiful thing I've ever seen, but I mustn't wear it now."

"Why not?"

"I want it to be my wedding ring, the only ring I'll ever wear. And I want you to have a matching one."

She removed it from her finger and gently placed it in his hand. He closed his fingers around it, simultaneously awed that this tantalizing creature had given her heart to him, while amused that she would never cease to be an enigma.

"I should go in now," he said reluctantly. "XT, Graeme and I are meeting with the contractor. Are you coming?"

"Not just yet," said Hilma. "I'd like to do a bit of daydreaming before I go in."

They kissed again, and while Garth made his way to the abbey, Hilma and the dogs waded through the deep grasses towards the recently discovered labyrinth. A short walk from where her feet touched upon the stones, she unexpectedly came upon the unburied upper portion of an abandoned oil holding tank. Peering through gaps in its weathered wooden lid, she saw that the tank contained oily dark water.

Here was a safety hazard she must bring to the attention of the others, she thought, changing direction to return to the abbey. She'd barely started back when she saw Claude approaching. She sighed, not in the mood to humour the lonely old guy. He was becoming a nuisance. Perhaps Sister Beatrice was right in insisting that he adapt more quickly to life away from the abbey.

"Good morning, Miss Moonstorey," he said, breathless from his hurried gait.

"Hello, Claude."

"Did you notice I called you Miss Moonstorey like Sister Beatrice ordered me to?"

Hilma nodded.

"I was joking," he explained.

"I figured that."

"You found one of our old holding tanks, I see," noted Claude, panting in his effort to keep pace with her quick steps.

"I wasn't expecting to find one in the labyrinth," she said.

"It's right in the middle, actually. The sisters built the labyrinth around it, trying to use the space creatively," said the former groundskeeper. "There were shrubs and flowers hiding it at one time."

"It will have to be drained before we can restore the labyrinth to its former state."

"I can make a permanent covering for it so there'll be no need to drain it," he said eagerly. "I have time on my hands now that the co-op students are gone. Dilly told me today that she won't be needing me after this week."

Not wanting to prolong the conversation by discussing safety issues, and unwilling to hurt his feelings by reminding him that he no longer worked for the sisters, Hilma said nothing.

"Hilma?"

"Yes?"

"I'm sorry about what happened," said Claude.

"Pardon?"

"I saw you return the ring and kiss him goodbye. I knew that cop wasn't right for you."

"What are you talking about?"

"Lucky I happened to be taking a break from helping Dilly and saw it all."

"Whatever you think you saw, Claude, you clearly misunderstood," said Hilma. "Garth and I are engaged to be married."

"But you returned the ring."

"I gave it to Garth for safe-keeping until our wedding day."

"So you were teasing me, pretending to like me, listening to me like you cared!" he said angrily. "I told you things I've never told another soul because you led me on."

Hilma's senses prickled with alarm. Silently, she called out to the dogs.

"You're evil like the others," he continued. "No better than a…a…a trollop!" He was spitting now in rage, his face contorted and blotchy.

When Hilma increased her pace, Claude roughly grabbed her arm.

"Don't walk away from me! Do you know what day it is?" he hissed menacingly.

Hilma tried to break free from the fierce grip of his fingers.

"It's All Hallows Eve," he said. "The perfect day to throw you in with the other whores who thought they were too good for me."

His hands were around her neck, painful and crushing. Unable to breathe, she struggled to fight him off. As she slipped into unconsciousness, Hilma was aware that all three spirit girls had gathered nearby, one holding a baby close to her breast. Then, through the darkness enveloping her, she heard a vicious growl and felt herself falling, falling...

Twenty-seven

All Saints Day blew in with gusts of rain under dark skies, hardly unusual for the first day of November. What was unusual was the yellow police tape cordoning off the back meadow of Black Springs Abbey. Dressed for the inclement weather, a police forensic team supervised the draining of the holding tank at the labyrinth's centre. Police vehicles, a van and several cruisers, were parked on the property.

By mid-afternoon, the holding tank was empty, exposing bones that, from visual inspection, belonged to two or three adults and at least one newborn infant. Around the same time, a second forensic unit dragging the pond at Bridgeview flats retrieved scattered bones buried in the mud and part of a shin bone tethered to a cement block.

Constable Garth brought the dreaded, though anticipated, news to the abbey. Dreaded, because the suspect in the crimes had lived most of his life at the abbey. Anticipated, because the man had already confessed.

The abbey's former groundskeeper was not, however, contrite. Under interrogation, he complained that he had been repeatedly humiliated and deceived by ungrateful tainted women who took advantage of the sisters' goodwill and his own trusting nature.

He told the police that his downfall began with his wife, Lorraine, an abbey penitent who didn't appreciate how lucky she was to marry him. Instead of being grateful, the woman had the nerve to flee with their infant son while he was hard at work one day.

He drove around until he found her at Creekside, cowering in the flats. When she resisted returning with him, he had no choice but to hit her with a tire iron and throw her beneath the covered bridge. Not knowing what to do with a baby, he turned his son over to the sisters for adoption.

Then there was Felicity, a pretty blonde penitent with a birthmark on her neck. She thought she was too good for him and rejected his kisses when he found her alone in the garden.

The third girl who earned his wrath was Corinne who repaid the good sisters by trying to run away with her baby. Naturally, he couldn't let her get away with it. And Myra, well, she had no business trying to stop him while he was dealing with Corinne. Besides, she was a witness and he couldn't let her leave the meadow.

"Those poor girls and the baby," said the abbess.

"Which baby are you talking about?" asked Sister Martha.

"I was thinking of Corinne's baby, but come to think of it, Claude's own baby was deprived of his mother's love. Who would have suspected that Claude, raised from childhood in this very abbey, would do such horrible things?"

"If it hadn't been for Shadow, God knows what would have happened to Hilma," said Sister Helen.

Sister Beatrice sat rigidly in her chair, her face ashen.

"Are you all right, Beatrice?" asked the abbess.

"I should have stopped him," she said in a strained voice.

"What are you saying?" asked Sister Colleen.

"I always suspected there was something wrong with Claude," said the organist. "That's why I was so strict with him. He was always sneaking around, spying on the girls, and it got worse after Lorraine left him. But even though he was especially skittish after each disappearance, I never believed him capable of such atrocities. It gave me quite a turn when Hilma told me about the ghosts."

"What ghosts?" asked the abbess.

"At one of our lessons, Hilma told me she'd been seeing spirit girls around the abbey and her descriptions matched girls who had been here as penitents, girls we thought had run away. Then, when I noticed Claude slinking around the abbey and finding excuses to be alone with Hilma when he had no business being here at all, I became frightened for her."

"Yet you said nothing to me," said the abbess.

Sister Beatrice wrung her hands. "I wasn't sure enough, but I tried to discourage all of you from letting him hang around here," she sniffed defensively.

"We thought you were just being especially difficult," said Sister Helen. "We're not mind readers, you know."

"You've been through a terrible ordeal, Hilma," said the abbess, turning her attention on her young assistant. "Are you alright?"

"I will be," said Hilma, her voice raspy from the assault.

She was wearing a scarf to hide the bruises and swelling on her neck. Yesterday morning, Garth, XT, and Graeme had rushed to her rescue after workmen became concerned enough about the persistent barking of both dogs to alert the porter. The men found Claude pinned to the ground by Shadow while Hilma lay limply nearby, Daisy at her side.

The police came for Claude who, already handcuffed by Garth, went meekly with the arresting officers. Hilma was carried upstairs to be attended to medically by Azur and XT. After spending most of the previous day and much of the current one in the infirmary, she insisted she was well enough to join the others.

"Do you want to tell the sisters about the ghost you saw at the flats?" suggested Azur. "It fits with Claude's confession that led the police to finding the bones near the Bridgeview Park bridge."

Hilma sent Garth a querying look, and he spoke on her behalf, telling them about the figure on the bridge with pale wavy hair who wore a flowered skirt and grey shawl. "Does it sound like Claude's wife?" he asked.

"The description fits," said Sister Beatrice, shaking her head ruefully. "To think I encouraged poor Lorraine to marry him."

"We all thought they'd be good for each other," said Sister Colleen. "Lorraine had no family to return to, and Claude was of marrying age. You can't blame yourself for that, Beatrice."

"Claude was never allowed to be a little boy," mused the abbess. "Everything was so rigid and proper in those days. If only we'd been more motherly with him as well as with the girls in our care."

"The focus was on morals, values and decorum," added Sister Helen.

They sat in silence until Sister Colleen rose, announcing it was time for her to prepare dinner. The novices excused themselves too, and soon everyone was moving about, allowing routine tasks to guide them through the remainder of the surreal day.

★ ★ ★

By the end of November, a semblance of order had been restored to the abbey. Forensics had identified the collected bone fragments from the tank as those of three young adult females and one newborn. The bones found beneath the bridge in the flats belonged to a young woman. After they had been photographed, x-rayed and categorized, they were delivered to the abbey in a wooden box. Following a solemn funeral service in the chapel, the remains were buried in the cloister cemetery, their spirits no longer roaming Black Springs Abbey.

The residents of the abbey bustled about preparing to move into their new accommodations. Responsible for hiring staff, Hilma recruited Eula to be receptionist and house mother of the forthcoming retreat house. In her new position, the writer would remain in her present suite as the sole permanent inhabitant of the second floor.

The day before moving into their condominium, Garth and Hilma were married in the abbey chapel in the presence of the entire community. Beguiling in a gown of lace and satin, her veil incorporated into a wreath of white and red silk flowers, the bride walked shyly up the aisle on the arm of her grandfather, Bram.

Preceding them were Azur, the maid of honour, and Meri who, dressed like a princess, solemnly held before her a beribboned satin cushion bearing two wedding bands. The smaller of the gold rings was encircled with tiny ruby and opal stones. The larger one had fewer, though larger, birthstones. The groom, elegant in his police dress uniform, awaited the procession from the front of the chapel in the company of his best man, Xavier Tennyson.

Unseen through the stain glass windows, snow began to fall outside, blanketing Black Springs Abbey in winter whiteness.

ABOUT THE AUTHOR

Gloria Pearson-Vasey is a storyteller who weaves magical realism and contemporary issues into her works of literary and science fiction, mystery and historical fantasy.

A member of The Writers' Union of Canada and Crime Writers of Canada, Pearson-Vasey's background includes nursing, psychology, music, journalism and theology. Inspired by her autistic son's unique sensory experiences, her writing reflects the hidden nature of things.

She lives in a picturesque Ontario town, enjoying nature, country drives, reading, and time with family.

Visit Gloria's website http://www.gloriapearsonvasey.com to discover more about her books.